PRAISE FOR
WHEN AUDREY MET ALICE

"Just the right amount of adventure, surprises, and fun that will leave you wanting more... An amusing and exciting story about life in the White House that translates to any girl who has ever felt left out. From heartwarming moments to LOL stitches, this book has it all."

—GirlsLife.com

"Teens will find Alice's wild diary entries outrageous and riveting... This book aims to inspire and stir young girls to unearth their inner Alice Roosevelt and to 'eat up the world.' A rowdy and winning addition."

—*School Library Journal*

"[An] entertaining debut... Details of life in the White House, combined with Audrey's more ordinary struggles will keep readers hooked."

—*Publishers Weekly*

"This charming debut brings Alice Roosevelt to life when thirteen-year-old "first daughter" Audrey finds Alice's century-old diary and turns to it for advice... An appealing journey and a fascinating life."

—*Kirkus Reviews*

"A terrific work of blended realistic and historical fiction... The combination of humor, history, light romance, and social consciousness make Rebecca Behrens's debut novel a winner."

—*BookPage*

"The juxtaposition of Audrey and Alice's stories creates an interesting counterpoint of past and present...the first-person narrative is consistently engaging. An enjoyable first novel."

—*Booklist*

"Rebecca Behrens combines charming and quirky characters from two different centuries, creating a believable, engaging story that tugs at the heart and tickles the funny bone."

—Nikki Loftin, award-winning author of
The Sinister Sweetness of Splendid Academy

"A fun look into the private life of an inspiring first daughter."

—Marissa Moss, bestselling author of the
Amelia's Notebook and Mira's Diary series

WHEN AUDREY MET ALICE

REBECCA BEHRENS

sourcebooks
jabberwocky

For Jane, who always told me to write,
and Jim, who always told me about TR

Sourcebooks and the colophon are registered trademarks of Sourcebooks, Inc.

Published by Sourcebooks Jabberwocky, an imprint of Sourcebooks, Inc.
P.O. Box 4410, Naperville, Illinois 60567-4410
(630) 961-3900
Fax: (630) 961-2168
www.jabberwockykids.com

Library of Congress Cataloging-in-Publication data is on file with the publisher.

Source of Production: Versa Press, East Peoria, Illinois, USA
Date of Production: March 2015
Run Number: 5003538

Printed and bound in the United States of America.
VP 10 9 8 7 6 5 4 3 2 1

Chapter 1

I t is ridiculously difficult to get a pizza delivered to 1600 Pennsylvania Avenue.

I raced down the hallway connecting the Residence to the East Wing, on my way to make sure that one of the staffers was ready to run out to the Northwest Gate and guide the delivery guy through visitor security, where the pizzas would be inspected and metal-detected. I passed the Family Theater on my way and poked my head inside. "Is the movie set up?"

My Uncle Harrison appeared from the projection booth in back. He'd flown out from the Midwest to help me throw my party. "Yup! We're just about to test it out."

"Awesome!" I did a little happy dance and then dashed out of the theater, back to searching for a pizza wrangler.

I don't exactly order a lot of pizzas around here—why would I, when I can wander down to the kitchen and get basically whatever food my heart desires? A mint-chocolate-chip sundae with a fresh-out-of-the-oven brownie? Sure! Vegetarian sushi rolls? Coming right up! French fries shaped like zoo animals? No problem!

But at every party I've attended since I started at Friends Academy, we've feasted on delivery pizza. Thanks to security and scheduling, I don't get to many parties these days. So once I *finally* had a chance to invite people over—the whole eighth-grade class of Friends—I wanted my party to be like all the others I'd missed. Well, as close as a party in the White House can be.

Last week, the studio making the *Aquatica* cyborg-mermaid trilogy into movies sent me an advance copy of the first film. (Getting advance copies of books and movies is one of the perks of being First Kid.) I had an amazing idea: *What if I hold a screening for my class, before the movie is even in theaters?*

The people in the East Wing office put in a few calls with the studio heads, and they agreed that I could screen the movie on the Tuesday before it opened. I couldn't send out my invite fast enough. "Movie Screening Party! Come over to my place and watch the *Aquatica* movie—before anyone but the stars themselves!" I wrote. Within an hour, everyone in my class replied yes. People were writing stuff like, "OMG! You're the best, Audrey" and "Coolest party ever." Even Madeline Horn was excited, and she has hated me ever since the election, because her grandfather was running for veep—and lost. This screening party wouldn't make up for the many, many social events I'd missed in the past year, but it would help.

I rounded a corner and almost collided with one of the staffers. My ballet flats squeaked as I skidded to a stop. My heart kept racing. "Do you know if the pizza is here?" My party's start time ticked closer.

The staffer said, "Not yet. But don't worry, Audrey—we're on it." I don't know what all *it* entails in terms of food security. I know if my parents and I go out to eat, we have to bring along our own bottled water and condiments, and someone from the Secret Service monitors our food as it's being made in the kitchen. An agent also washes our plates and cutlery before the food is put on them and watches the dishes like a hawk as they are brought out to the table. When we are at 1600 (I still can't call it "my house"), my mom doesn't have a taster—someone to take a bite of her food before she starts eating to make sure it won't make her sick. But other food-security specifics are a mystery, even to me. For all I know, pizza that I'm going to eat has to be supervised too. Maybe one of my agents spent the afternoon at Pizzeria Paradiso, wearing a floppy chef's hat (with the radio earpiece sticking out) and helping spin the pie dough in the air. Maybe I should check their suits for telltale flour smudges.

The staffer smiled and put her hand on my shoulder reassuringly. "Why don't you head back to the Visitors Foyer and supervise decorations?" I guess she picked up on my nervousness. As excited as I was to see the new movie with all my classmates, I worried about everything going smoothly. When it came to socializing outside school, I was rusty.

I skipped back to the foyer and rearranged the cardboard cutouts of the movie's stars that the studio had sent along with the film. My guests could pose for pictures with them. *I bet by tomorrow these cutouts will be in 50 percent of my class's profile pics.* I straightened the napkins on the table and took a few test sips of the special blue *Aquatica* punch the chefs had created for the screening. It tasted like fizzy lemonade, and it was delicious. A row of clamshells made out of oranges decorated the rim of the bowl. I admired the tiny marzipan mermaids on the dessert table. The clock showed it was 6:15 p.m. People would start arriving any minute. I sat down in an armchair and surveyed the room, grinning. *Everything is perfect.* It was one of those moments in which I couldn't believe that this was my *life* now, throwing movie-screening parties for my friends in the *White House*. Now my racing heart wasn't from nervousness, but excitement.

"Audrey! Audrey!" My uncle's voice, tinged with panic, came from the direction of the Family Theater. My first thought was, *The projector broke the movie.* As I started to stand up from my seat, I saw Harrison running down the hall, flanked by my agents, Hendrix and Simpkins. Harrison's face was white as a sheet, and both agents wore grim frowns. Hendrix swept over and put her arm around my shoulders, pulling me with her as she hustled us out of the foyer and back into the Residence.

"What's happening? Where are we going?" At that point I felt more confused than scared.

Simpkins piped up from behind me. "Security breach. We'll explain in a minute, but first we need to get you guys downstairs."

"But my party! People are going to start showing up any minute!" Simpkins and Hendrix exchanged a look but didn't say anything. I turned to look at Harrison and tried to hold my ground, but Hendrix kept pulling me forward. Harrison wasn't any help; he looked like he was going to barf, which in turn made my stomach drop. Harrison's the opposite of my mom, and whenever possible he refuses to take anything seriously. I've never seen him worried, not even the time we set a tablecloth on fire making crème brûlée. To see him rattled was creepy.

"Is this for a fence jumper?" I asked. We get those a lot, actually. The agents on the grounds and the infrared sensors pick them up right away, and the people are usually confused or crazy but harmless. The Secret Service doesn't bother to bring me and my parents into secure areas when that happens.

All Simpkins said was, "No." My stomach dropped to the sub-basements.

The ground floor of the Residence bustled with staff on walkie-talkies and guards running around, and suddenly I was terrified. "Where's my mom? Where's my dad?"

Hendrix squeezed my shoulder in a running hug. "They're still on their way home, but they're fine, sweetie."

Once we were in the basement, Harrison and I got someone to tell us what was going on: a small plane was in the no-fly zone, and it wasn't responding to air-traffic control. When the situation unfolded, the Secret Service decided to keep my dad at his lab at Johns Hopkins University, and my mom stayed somewhere secure in the Capitol building. Harrison and I sat in stony silence as I compulsively twirled my hair. I get so worried about something happening to my mom or dad, and I wished they were here with us. My stomach clenched, and I felt like I was going to be sick. I squeezed my eyes shut and pictured my parents safe at home. Our Minnesota home.

We waited in the basement for what felt like *forever* until some military-looking guy declared the situation all clear. Turns out the plane, an itty-bitty Cessna, was being flown by a student pilot. The poor guy got lost, didn't know about the no-fly zone, and couldn't figure out how to work the radio to explain what was going on. It had been worrisome enough that the fighter planes went up, but thankfully nobody got hurt. Color returned to Harrison's face immediately upon hearing all that.

He coughed and smiled sheepishly. "That'll get your heart rate going. Right, Audi?" The fact that he was back to using his nickname for me meant he'd fully recovered. I still felt like a wrung-out dishrag.

"Sure." My legs were shaky from the running and the stress, but I stood up anyway. "We need to get back to the party, Harrison." I wondered which early birds were standing around in the foyer, waiting for their host to show. I stretched and headed for the stairs.

"Audrey," Simpkins said, stopping me from heading up. "I have bad news. We're following protocol. The security level has been elevated for the rest of the day. I'm afraid you know what that means." Simpkins's face crumpled into a frown. "No nonessential guests. You can't have the screening anymore."

"No!" I shouted. A few staffers glanced over at us. "They can't do that!" I shook my head. "No way." I could feel hot tears forming, but I fought them back. *They can't do this to me. Not today. Not for my party.*

"I'm sorry, Audrey. They have to. No visitors at level red. Your guests were already turned away at the gate."

I covered my face with my hands. "I'm going to die. I'm going to die of embarrassment. I am letting the entire eighth grade down." More than that, I'd been trying to have people over for *months*. I was so disappointed and dejected that I wanted to sink to the bottom of the White House swimming pool and stay there forever.

"There's no way an exception can be made?" Harrison crossed his arms over his chest. "This party means a great deal to Audrey." I think he also didn't want to miss a chance to watch the movie. Harrison loves the trilogy as much as I do—maybe more. He was even wearing a Team Mermaid T-shirt under his pullover.

Simpkins shook his head. "I'm sorry, but no." I ran up the stairs, those tears now streaming down my face.

An hour later, Harrison and I sat in the front row of the Family Theater, watching the movie before anyone else in the country. Just the two of us. On a table next to Harrison was a carafe of beautiful blue punch and a plate of those marzipan mermaids, and next to still-sniffling me was a box of tissues. Oh, and a dozen pizza boxes were stacked at our feet. At least the pizza guy made it before the lockdown.

Chapter 2

Every weekday afternoon, at 3:55 p.m. on the dot, Simpkins leads me to the idling car, waits for the signal from Hendrix at the wheel, and ushers me inside. He does a visual check of the surroundings before opening the passenger door and taking his place next to Hendrix. They lock the doors, then Simpkins grunts into his walkie-talkie, "Tink on board. All clear?" He waits for a staticky message from somewhere inside 1600, then nods to Hendrix. "We're ready to roll." The routine is like something my dance teacher back in St. Paul could've choreographed.

The day after my ill-fated party, I stretched out onto the cool leather seat and stared out the window. My classmates milled around outside school. No yellow buses waited to pick them up—it's not that kind of school—but instead a crowd of fancy black SUVs and luxury sedans, all with tinted windows. Before heading off to Mandarin lessons or field-hockey practice, everyone else gets to spend a little more time hanging out, doing normal after-school stuff. I watch them from behind mirrored, bulletproof glass.

Our car pulled away and sped down the long, tree-lined driveway. I shifted in my seat, craning my neck to watch Friends Academy disappear from view. "Friends Academy, my butt," I muttered.

When my parents and I moved to Washington last December, we spent lots of time visiting classrooms and lunching with boring, crusty trustees to choose my new school. Eventually, we picked Friends Academy because when I visited, I saw smiling kids running around the leafy campus, smiling kids hanging out in the science labs, and smiling kids tuning instruments in their fancy concert hall. A lot of those smiling kids had important parents too— journos and diplomats and senators—so it couldn't be that hard to blend in, right? It *looked* like everyone was friendly at Friends.

Well, looks can be deceiving. Friends Academy: not so friendly.

I stretched out my arm and pressed my fingertips against the cold window glass, thinking about something I'd overheard in French class. *Everyone is going tonight,* said Madeline, talking about the consolation-prize outing to *Aquatica. Well, everyone except* Fido, *who already saw it.* Then she rolled her eyes. I'd never heard the term *Fido* before, but

I didn't need a degree in linguistics to figure out to what, or whom, it probably referred. Was that why Alexander Wade had *woof*ed at me in the hall the other day?

I planned to get out of Friends as fast as possible after last period, but my one actual friend, Quint, stood slumped up against my locker when I ran up to it.

"Bummer about the party, Audrey. But I know it's not your fault they canceled it," he said as I sprinted up and started spinning the combination lock.

I offered him a half-smile. "I'm going to beg for home-schooling. It's been that kind of a day." I pulled my books out and shoved them in my bag.

"People are superhard on you with stuff like that." Quint shook his head, causing his brown curls to wave around his face. "It's not cool."

I bit my lip, wondering if I should ask him. "Quint—what's *Fido*?"

He paused. "A clichéd name for a dog," he finally replied, refusing to look me in the eye.

"It's me, right? Madeline has people referring to me like I'm a dog now? Is that it?" I felt more hot tears forming in my eyes, which I willed to stop.

"No, no, it's not like that. It's an acronym; like, *Fido* is *eff-doh*, as in F-D-O-T-U-S. First Daughter of the United States. Nobody's calling you a dog, Audrey. I swear." Quint reached out as though he was going to hug me, but then glanced over at my beefy, six-foot, dark-sunglasses-wearing Secret Service agents. (Well, it's mean to call Hendrix beefy—but she *is* ripped, and tall, and with those shades on she sure looks tough.)

Quint dropped his arm to his side. "I promise you it's a friendly nickname."

"It still sucks. Nicknames are one thing; secret nicknames are another. Especially if they sound like dog names," I glowered. "You have to admit that's jerky."

Quint shook his head. "I think it's meant like a code name. You know, like whatever those guys"—he motioned to Hendrix—"use for you." *Tink* is what they use for me. I picked it from the list of names they gave our family, all starting with the letter *T*. Hendrix told me it was a good choice because I look like the Disney version of Tinkerbell: short, with bangs and blond hair that I wear in a lazy ballerina bun all the time. Plus, Hendrix said, "You're a little… spirited, just like Tinkerbell." I think that might be a nice way of saying that I'm hyper and/or moody.

"It still means that people are talking about me when I'm not there," I whined.

Quint snorted. "Come on, Audrey. Did you really ever think they weren't?"

I grudgingly nodded, knowing it was true. Lesson #1

about being First Kid: Someone is always talking about you or your mom. It's been that way ever since she first announced her campaign.

Traffic wasn't bad, at least for the Beltway, and soon I was back to 1600. I ran upstairs, and I flung myself facedown on my bedspread, dropping my messenger bag with a thud on the floor. I inhaled the familiar fabric-softener smell and ran my fingers across the nubby fabric, pretending for a minute that I was back home in Minnesota. I hadn't brought any of my furniture with me to Washington, but I brought all of my stuff, including my bedspread, billion yellow pillows, faded plush rug, and all of my framed pictures. Now when I go back to St. Paul I'm shocked at the bare walls and stripped-down bed. The house I'd lived in all my life isn't really my home anymore.

It hadn't been a *home* for a while—while my mom was on the campaign trail, my dad won that huge grant and had to come out to Johns Hopkins to set up his fancy new lab. He flew home most weekends, but then we usually spent them campaigning with my mom. I wound up staying in Wisconsin with Uncle Harrison and his partner, Max, for a few months before the election. It'd been a while since I felt like I had a place of my own, where I was free to do whatever I wanted. I missed that.

I rolled over and stared at the ceiling. The cracks in the

Rebecca Behrens

paint looked like the veins on leaves. That's another surprising thing about 1600—the White House isn't all that lavish, at least in the Residence. It's a fancy building but a super-old one, and in places it looks its age. Something about being a historic site and belonging to the federal government makes renovations tricky. Though my room, the "Yellow Bedroom," isn't bad. It has buttery yellow walls—yellow's my favorite color—and a nice view. Chelsea Clinton, another White House only child, lived in it.

I turned onto my side to look at my alarm clock. It read 5:00 p.m., so Kim would probably be home from running club. I grabbed the phone and dialed out. The phone rang four times before someone in the Mehrotra residence picked up.

"Hello?" It was Kim, slightly breathless.

"First Friend! How was practice?" I decided after the election that Kim needed a title too—she's been my best friend since kindergarten, after all. I even made her a "First Friend" T-shirt with the White House seal on it for her birthday last year.

"It kicked my butt. Big time. Can you hear me wheezing?"

"Whatevs, you know you're going to run in the Olympics someday. What's up?"

"Omigod, so much. Did I tell you about the dance last weekend?"

"Kim, I do still have Facebook, you know. I might not be at Hamilton but I'm online. All the time, actually." That's true; I've considered making a "First Friend" decal for my laptop too.

"Doy. I meant, did I tell you about all the *drama*?"

"No, but I want to hear all about it." I paused. "Did Paul go?" I crossed my fingers.

Kim paused before answering. "He did. With Tessa."

I sucked in a deep breath, and I swear I could feel my heart aching as my chest expanded with air. Paul had been *my* crush, for years. And Tessa had been my friend. "That's cool." My voice only cracked a little. "I don't really have a crush on him anymore anyway." Not exactly true. I was trying to sound very mature and Zen about it—the opposite of how I felt. I felt like punching a hole through one of my historic walls.

"Oh, good." Kim sounded relieved. "Enough about boring old Hamilton. How're you?"

"Mch. Yesterday was supposed to be my movie screening party. But the Secret Service canceled it after a security breach." I heard Kim gasp, so before she could freak out, I added, "It was a false alarm, but you know they take those way seriously."

"Thank goodness. But boo to canceling your party."

"Harrison and I still watched it, with way more punch

and pizza than two people need. Everybody else decided to see the movie tonight, without me. Madeline arranged it."

"Rude!" I'd complained to Kim about Madeline's unwavering iciness many times.

"I also I found out my darling classmates refer to me as 'Fido.' You know, like a *dog*." I shuddered. "Except they think it's some kind of clever shorthand for *First Daughter*. Quint clued me in."

"That sucks, *Fido*," Kim teased. "But I'm sure they don't use it in a mean way. Remind me, who's Quint? Is *he* why you don't have a crush on Paul anymore?"

"Just a guy from my music class." Picturing Quint, especially his bright, brown eyes and toothy grin, made me smile. "He's cool."

"That's great!" Kim said, a little too cheerily. "Listen, I hate to do this, but I gotta go. If I finish my science homework, my mom is taking me and Tessa to Mickey's Diner. Carbo-loading before the 5K, you know." I closed my eyes and pictured the familiar, red vinyl counter stools that my friends and I loved to spin around on while we watched the cooks fry up our food. I could almost taste the pancakes. I felt an unwelcome pang of homesickness for St. Paul.

"Okay, I'll let you go. I got a package of books again anyway. Advance copies of the new trilogy by the *Aquatica* lady about ninja centaurs. Well, the first book."

"You have to send one to me when you're done! See? There are perks to your new house."

Kim was right. We hung up, and I leaned back into my bed, letting the receiver progress from silence to dial tone to screeching. I couldn't get rid of the image of all my old friends hanging out without me. It felt like being excluded on the playground, except I couldn't fault any of them for it. I might have stayed on my bed indefinitely, but the door to my room whipped open.

"Oh! Miss Audrey, I didn't think you were in here." It was one of the housekeeping staff, Janet, come to collect my school uniform. Dirty clothes usually last about five minutes in 1600 before someone whisks them away—it sometimes feels like the employees simply hang around waiting for me, my mom, or dad to put down a coffee cup or shed a cardigan. It drives me insane because I feel like someone's always watching me.

"I haven't changed yet. If you just give me a sec—" I started to shrug out of my navy blazer.

"No, no, no! I'll be back when you're at dinner. Don't trouble yourself, dear." With that, Janet ducked out and shut the door.

"Do I *ever* get a minute to myself in this place?" I sputtered as I rolled off my lofted bed. *So much for the privacy of my room.* I ripped off my uniform clothes and threw on some sweats. Clean, fresh, fabric softener–scented sweats that someone had washed in the past forty-eight hours. I wished that I could smell three-days-old pajama pants or slept-in sheets for a change, like a normal person.

❧

"Debra! You are not going to believe the day I had," I exclaimed as I bounded into the kitchen. My favorite place in 1600 is nothing like our kitchen at home—a spacious, sunny room with vintage red-and-white floral wallpaper, scuffed white cupboards and cabinets, and a cork floor. The White House kitchen is cramped and industrial, with pots and pans and high-tech light fixtures hanging over long stainless-steel tables. I think you'd need an advanced engineering degree just to turn on some of the fancy-schmancy ovens. Probably because the kitchen's so dinky, there's a separate sub-room just for refrigeration and a chocolate shop across the hall, where all the pastries and desserts for big State Dinners are made. I love the chocolate shop, which smells like an Easter basket year-round. Especially wonderful is the "cookie jar," which is actually a big, rolling container with twenty types of cookies inside. Debra, one of the chefs, showed me where they keep the keys for it. When she's on duty, though, she insists on making me ones from scratch. One of my first evenings in the White House, I had wandered downstairs and asked for a snack. Debra had pulled out a bag of chocolate chips and some flour before I finished my request.

"You don't need to make anything—an Oreo would be fine," I'd said. I didn't want to trouble her.

She'd shaken her head. "Nuh-uh. Baking cookies is still my favorite culinary activity, despite studying at the CIA. Although, I can whip up a killer soufflé."

"The CIA? Like, in Langley?" *Spies use soufflés to kill people? Shouldn't that be secret?*

"Oh, no," Debra had laughed. "The chef CIA, not the spy one. Culinary Institute of America in New York. That's where I learned to be a pastry chef."

"Ha. That makes a little more sense." I had smiled, imagining Debra as a cookie-baking spy. The superfast oven already had filled the room with the scent of butter and chocolate chips. It'd reminded me of home, and I had savored that familiar, happy twinge. Debra, and her cookies, quickly became my favorite thing about life at 1600.

The night after my nonparty, she had enough pots and pans going that I knew she was making food for more than one. "Am I not eating alone tonight?" Many nights, I did— either in the kitchen while chatting with Debra, or up in my room while watching TV.

"Not tonight, sweetness. Your parents are on their way home, so you can eat with them." Debra looked up from the vegetables she was chopping. The knife was whipping up and down in a controlled frenzy. Perhaps you *could* train a spy at culinary school.

"Seriously? I'm not Little Orphan Audrey tonight? Cool." *Now if only my parents would check their phones at the door. Unlikely.*

"Nope. Brace yourself for quality time with your parental units."

"Did I hear myself referred to as a 'parental unit'?" My dad walked into the kitchen behind us. He was still wearing his lab coat, embroidered with JEFFREY RHODES, MD/PHD.

"Dad! You're actually home!" I hopped up to give him a hug. He smelled like lab soap.

He ruffled my hair. "You'd think I'd been in Antarctica, not at Hopkins." My dad's research is on cancer treatment, and his grant was for an experiment on a protein called p53. So far, it looks like the mice in his lab with the p53 gene can fight off malignant tumors, which could be a huge breakthrough for human treatment. Sometimes Dad spends days at a time holed up at Hopkins, monitoring the progress. "First Gent" activities are squeezed into his downtime. Same with parental stuff. Sadly, I think the only way I could get more time to spend with him would be if I wore a mouse costume and pretended to be one of his subjects.

"You might as well be there. I think the last time I saw you, I still had braces."

"Hey, now—I know you've been rid of metal mouth for months."

We went upstairs to the Family Residence Dining Room and sat down at the place settings some silent employee had whisked onto the table before we entered. My dad reached for his briefcase on autopilot and opened it, then stopped short of pulling out some lab reports and clamped it back shut. Maybe he sensed me glaring at the briefcase. "Tell me about your day while we wait for Mom."

"Well, right now my whole class is at the movies together. Without me."

My dad pressed his glasses back up the bridge of his nose and examined me. "Bummer. But you and Harrison still got to see it before opening night, right? That's pretty nifty."

Before I could respond, the door opened and my mom strode into the room, trailed by several aides and her chief of staff, Denise Colbert. Mom was nodding and *mmm-hmmm*ing as she finished signing several documents that the aides were holding in front of her. She stood up and pushed her silvery-blond hair, cut in a signature bob, behind one ear.

"What about the statement regarding the gay-marriage legislation being proposed, Madam President? Are you ready to promote a stance on the issue? The special-interest groups are waiting." Denise shoved another fat memo folder in front of my mom.

Mom shook her head and passed it back to Denise, unopened. "I thought we discussed that this is a low-priority issue for now. I can't afford to distract anyone from the peace summit or the energy initiatives." I frowned. It isn't low priority for some people, including Harrison and Max. I opened my mouth to say something, but my dad motioned to zip it. He never used to do that—my parents always encouraged me to share my opinions at the dinner table.

My mom smiled as Denise stuck the folder into her over-stuffed attaché case. "We'll get to it, eventually. Now if you'll excuse me, I'm overdue for a family dinner."

Denise had already swept over to stand beside my dad's chair, hovering like a vulture. "Jeffrey, I'd like to speak with you about school visits that we need representation at this month. I already spoke to Susan." Susan Pierpont is my dad's chief of staff. "Perhaps you can give me a call after dinner?" Denise never turns off work mode. I'm convinced that she works even while she sleeps, that the dream version of Denise composes emails and drafts memos and writes meeting agendas during every REM cycle.

"Why don't we set up the dates right now?" My dad stood up from his chair and started conferring with Denise. I swear, getting my whole family to sit down together is like herding cats.

My mom, out of her staffers' clutches, sat down at her place and smiled at me. "Hi, dear." She reached across the table and squeezed my hand. Her heavy-lidded eyes betrayed the chronic tiredness her makeup artist works so hard to hide. She looked way older than she used to, but I knew better than to tell her that. "How are you doing?"

"Decent. How's, um, the country doing today?"

She laughed. "It's doing fine." My dad sat back down at the table. Like clockwork, a kitchen employee materialized from behind the doors with plates full of food. Just a normal night at the Rhodes family dinner table, if eating scalloped potatoes at 1600 Pennsylvania Avenue can ever be considered normal. And if I can't consider it normal, I doubt anyone else can.

Chapter 3

F riends Academy is too *fancy* to have a normal bell. Instead, a recording of the theme from Mozart's Sonata in C major tells us when fifty-five minutes are up. "Mozart stimulates the brain," the smarmy guide had explained during my tour. Whether or not that's true, I think using music as a bell is pretty cool; my public school in Minnesota used your typical earsplitting buzzer.

On Friday when Mozart started wafting out the speakers at the end of second period, I lingered around my desk until the other kids filed out of the room. French class had been *odieux*. During small-group conversation practice, my partners, Stacia and Claire (who happen to be Madeline's besties), refused to talk about anything but the *fête* at Madeline's country house the coming weekend. Of course, she hadn't invited me. I fiddled with my charm bracelet and tried to act like I wasn't listening to the conversation. "*Vas-tu à la fête*, Audrey?" asked Stacia.

"*Je ne peux pas*," I replied. I hung my head and flipped to the index of my textbook as though I was looking for something. *Is it too late to switch to independent-study Mandarin?* The fewer classes with Madeline and her minions, the better.

Quint was waiting outside the room when I slunk out at the tail end of the sonata snippet. "Who died, Rhodes?"

I secretly love that he calls me by my last name. That is a good type of pet name for someone (in contrast to *Fido*). "My soul, a little." I heaved my bag over my right shoulder. "Why—is it that obvious I'm miserable?"

"To me, maybe. Your mouth is doing its frowny-face thing, you know, when you're not exactly frowning but you'd like to be. Also, you're superslouchy." Quint smiled and continued before I could think of some snappy comeback. "Which is weird for you. What's wrong?" *How does he know so much about my posture and facial expressions?* Thinking about Quint thinking about *me* made my heart flutter.

"Madeline's *fête* this weekend, which I wasn't invited to. Not that I could go, anyway. I think there's a State Dinner or something."

"I probably can't either," Quint shrugged. "My parents are kinda strict about parties. I was only going to beg if you were going." He quickly added, "You know, because you don't go to a lot of parties."

I blushed and muttered thanks. I was glowing inside, knowing that he wanted me to be there.

Everyone wanted to be around me when I first started at Friends. Some kids still do. It freaks me out, actually. I'd been popular back in St. Paul—a comfortable kind of popular, without social-climbing drama or anything. I've known all of my Minnesota friends since preschool and so with them my mother's political rise wasn't weird. Politics was simply what my mom did, like how Kim's dad is chancellor at UM and Tessa's mom is a Target exec and Paul's dad runs the newspaper. In DC, I can tell just by the way people look at me—the way their eyes search my face, like they are trying to see my mom in it—that they are more interested in my family than me.

A week after starting school, my parents arranged a party at the White House for all fifty kids in my class. (All classes at Friends have exactly fifty students—no more and no less—so I'm the odd-duck fifty-first student in my class.) Everyone came except Quint, who was out of town. We took a tour, swam in the White House pool, and ate incredible food that Debra and the rest of the executive dining team had whipped up. I kept walking up to kids at the party and trying to start a conversation.

"Hi, I'm Audrey. I don't think we've met," I said to Alexander Wade.

"Cool, I'm Alexander. Can I see the Lincoln Bedroom?"

Or to Naveen: "Hi, Naveen! I'm glad you could make it."

"Yeah, me too. So are we going to get to hang out here all the time? Where's the Situation Room?"

I understood why everyone was excited about being in 1600, but I got a bit annoyed that they seemed more interested in finding the Oval Office than meeting me.

So I hadn't made many friends other than Quint. He was my lab partner in science my first semester at Friends, and he never seemed to care that I was no longer a normal person. Maybe that's because his parents are big deals too: his dad is the U.S. ambassador to the United Nations and his mom is an important professor at Howard University. Lately I *have* developed the teensiest little crush on Quint, but there's no way I'll act on it. The logistics of me having a boyfriend are too complicated. For example, when Chelsea Clinton lived here, the Secret Service chaperoned all of her dates; I could expect at least the same. *Awkward.*

"Earth to Audrey," Quint said, waving his hand in front of my face. "Seriously, you look upset."

"It's nothing. Nobody else needs to wallow in misery with me." I paused. "But I have to admit I like having you for company."

"Then I shall call you Misery, because you love my company."

I punched his arm. "Dork!"

"Watch it, Misery!" Quint laughed as he grabbed my hands. His palms were full of calluses from playing the drums, but his fingertips were soft and smooth. I tried to jerk out of his grasp, giggling as he held his grip. We stayed like that for a few minutes, until I heard an *ahem* behind us. I turned and saw Agent Simpkins tapping his watch. Mozart started playing his final warning, meaning passing time was almost up. Quint dropped my hands like a hot dish.

"I should go to class. See you in music history?"

"But of course," Quint bowed in a sarcastic chivalrous display (probably for Simpkins's benefit), then turned and ran off down the hall.

My heart pounded in my chest as I took my seat in science class. Mei, my benchmate, smiled as she pushed her notebooks to the side. She'd been hinting that her older brother wanted a West Wing internship for weeks. I tried to focus on my lab notebook, but I still felt amped up. I replayed the scene in my head: Quint grabbing my hands in his and pulling me toward him. I liked having his hands hold mine. I shivered as I pictured his face smiling down at me. Quint was pretty tall, and he towered over me. That was another thing that I liked. I couldn't wipe the hint of a smile from my face.

It reminded me of what life used to be like, in Minnesota, when I'd had plenty of friends, including a crush with serious potential. Paul Clausen of the sparkling blue eyes, few zits, and white-blond hair. He loved to hike at Itasca and wanted to become a large-animal vet. He had known me since kindergarten and didn't care that my mom was a politician. I know Paul liked me too, and it seemed inevitable that we'd start going out. And then the campaign happened, and things got weird and then I moved.

I hadn't felt anything like what I used to feel around Paul until today. Somehow, Quint holding my hands…it was stupid, but I felt a sliver of that giddiness again. *But what good could come of liking Quint?* I couldn't risk jeopardizing my one real friendship in DC with a crush. *He'd get tired of all my First Daughter drama, and forget about me like Paul did. Plus, Denise would totally freak out about me dating because she tries to act like I am still a little kid.* She even thought that my jazz dance involved too much "gyrating" and that I needed to switch to ballet. A First Boyfriend was totally not part of her perfect public image for my family. Conclusion: Boyfriends are what normal people with normal lives have—not *Fidos*.

After dinner I brought my nightly cookie fix to my room and settled in with a good book. After a couple of hours of reading, I glanced at the clock and saw that it was only 10:00 p.m. I had that itchy feeling I'd been getting a lot lately, like the walls of my room were slowly closing in and my clothes were too tight and there wasn't enough air left for me to take a deep breath. *Time for some tea.* I shut my book and hopped up off the rug. I had a box of lavender chamomile somewhere in the Family Kitchen. I padded down the short hallway to the kitchen, pulled out the teapot, filled it up, and set it on the stovetop.

While I waited for it to whistle, I wandered into the Family Residence Dining Room. Seriously, there are as many dining rooms in 1600 as members of my family: the State Dining Room, Family Dining Room, and the Family Residence Dining Room. Plus, in warm weather we can eat up on the Promenade or take breakfast in the Solarium. Whenever my family eats together we eat in this dining room, but I hadn't poked around its nooks and crannies—even during the traditional scavenger hunt that the staff hosted for me and my Minnesota friends right after we moved in. I wandered around, stopping to open an ornately carved door, which to my disappointment only led to a closet. Once upon a time, this room had been a bedroom too. Another room type that 1600 has way too many of, at least for my family of three.

The closet was empty but for some boxes, and I started to push them aside, wondering what was in them. Books, maybe? One got caught on a plank of wood that was raised higher than the rest. *You'd think they'd have higher standards for carpentry in the White House.* When the box finally came free, I noticed that the plank was a slightly different color than the others, lighter and smoother but not varnished. I bent down to look more closely at it. There was something written on the short end of the piece. I kneeled down and wiped the dust and crud off it, revealing a crude inscription. It looked like it said, EAT UP THE WORLD, 1903.

I sat back on my heels, wondering why someone would use a written-on piece of wood to patch the floor in the White House. *Unless that was intentional, duh.* The way the plank was raised—I could pry it out, maybe. I slid my fingernails under the raised edges—*So long, purple nail polish*—and pulled. Nothing. I pushed down as hard as I could on the un-raised side of the plank, and voilà! The raised edge popped up a little higher. When I tried prying at it again, it grudgingly snapped up and away from the rest of the floor, releasing a little cloud of dust.

Coughing, I set the wood aside and peered into the small hole in the floor. I could see red-and-white checked fabric, some sort of little bundle. I hesitated before reaching into the gaping hole, hovering my hand above while summoning

32

up the nerve. Then I quickly reached in before I could imagine what gross stuff could be lurking in between the floorboards. I grasped the bundle and pulled it out, shaking the dust off. It was tied tightly shut, so I had to pick at the knot until the edges of the fabric spilled onto the floor. *What's inside? It better not be bones or dried blood, or I will puke all over this room.*

In the middle of what looked like an old handker-chief laid a few old postcards, each with tinted pictures of the same girl; a small, fat leather book; and a pack of cigarettes, unopened. I grabbed the cigarettes, which were some brand I'd never heard of, "Murad." Everything about the package looked old-timey, from the artwork to the script boasting "finest Turkish tobacco leaf." I set the pack down and gingerly picked up the first hand-tinted postcard, being careful of the frayed scalloped edges. The lady on it had an old-fashioned hairstyle and beautiful, piercing blue eyes. She stood in the middle of a garden or a jungle, with lush plants sticking out all around her. Her hands were clasped behind her back, lips pursed, and she looked down at the camera in a formal pose, although her eyes twinkled like she was about to laugh. Her clothes were Victorian-ish. I flipped over the card. On the back, it read: *Alice Roosevelt in the White House Conservatory, 1902.* I quickly flipped through the other postcards; they were of her too, and one image was labeled "Princess Alice." *Holy crap, holy crap!* I recognized the name—Alice was a former First Daughter. Really former. Teddy Roosevelt was POTUS back at the beginning of the 1900s. *No. Freaking. Way. Is this Alice Roosevelt's stuff?* My hands trembled a little as I finally picked up the leather book. I had a suspicion that it wasn't a book but a journal, and although I'm not sure why, I really wanted that hunch to be correct.

I fiddled with the clasp, but the whistling of the teapot startled me. I cursed at it and hurried into the kitchen, filled my huge mug, and ran back to the closet, hot tea sloshing all around. While the tea cooled, I took another look at the contents of the bundle. Right away, I noticed the embroidery on the corner of the handkerchief. CONGRATULATIONS. YOU HAVE AN APPETITE FOR LIFE. YOUR REWARD? MY WORDS.

"So I guess Alice Roosevelt, or whoever left this, wanted it to be found," I murmured. Gingerly, I picked up the journal. The rusted metal clasp on it opened easily now, to my delight. I carefully flipped through and saw that all of the pages were filled with a cramped, slanted handwriting. *How the heck does anyone read script like this?* I could barely make out the dates for some entries—1901, 1902. Glancing at the inside cover, clearer handwriting said:

The Diary of Alice Lee Roosevelt
Intensely Private Contents. No Peeking.

"Alice Lee! We have the same middle name and initials. So. Awesome," I whispered. Then I ignored the "no peeking" part and started deciphering the first entry immediately.

September 26, 1901
Dear Diary,

Now that I am the president's daughter, it seems like I ought to keep a diary. For the sake of remembering these momentous years, even though I think diaries are rather silly things. They're like writing letters to nobody, which seems like a waste of precious time. I have failed miserably at keeping a journal in the past. I will try better this time; perhaps more interesting things will happen to me now.

The lot of us just arrived at the "White House," which is the newly official name of this hulking white-washed presidential shack. I'm glad that we aren't calling it the "Executive Mansion" anymore. That moniker takes on more airs than the building merits; I dare say it's not a true mansion. When I first visited it as a little girl, grizzled President Benjamin Harrison bent down and told me it was his "jail." Heh. This positively grim building somewhat resembles one—it's far from lavish. Crumbling walls, leaks, peeling paint, and decrepit furnishings. There are not nearly enough bathrooms on the second floor, at least for a family of eight. My stepmother will have her hands full fixing up the place, as per her First Lady duties. As though she didn't already have her hands full with my rambunctious siblings, and me!

Now the White House is full of young people and overrun it we shall. Ted, Kermit, Ethel, Archie, Quentin, and I have already discovered endless possibilities for mischief and merriment. Last night, we took some tin trays from the pantry and found them excellent as sleds on the stairs leading down to the main hallway. It was our Inauguration of Fun. That was, until Archie knocked his head on the banister and wailed like bloody murder. Stepmother wasn't pleased at that. She isn't pleased with much right now, between all the mourning for President McKinley and even more mourning for our family's precious "privacy." If she hated attention so, she had no business marrying Theodore Roosevelt.

All of us are all excited, though. I hope being the children of the president will make life in Washington grand, even though I know from personal experience that this town can be like a little Puritan village, at least when compared to life in bustling New York City. It will be far better than Albany, where we lived while my father was governor. Albany was dreadfully boring. The places one is forced to live when one's father is such an Important Man! (And now he is the Most Important Man.)

Whenever we travel with Father, we create a whirling ruckus. Crowds and press and attention from all corners of the earth. I rather love the feel of it, but then again, I am someone who wants to eat up the world. I expect that I will be able to eat more of it now, for two reasons: (1) Being the eldest in my family, I expect freedom to do as I please here. The addition of a few security men to guard my father and our family should not hamper that. (And after the tragic assassination of McKinley, they are indeed necessary.) My father has a Secret Service man who is with him all the time, William Craig, and another one, Sloane, watches the little boys as they scamper around. But the rest of us don't see much of the Service at home. I don't mind when I do—most of the chaps are good sports. (2) I expect to have my society debut this year and I will get to have it in the White House. It doesn't get more exciting than that, does it?

I am supposed to be unpacking my hatboxes and such now. More later.

To Thine Own Self Be True,

Alice

P.S. That Shakespearean allusion is my newly adopted motto for life, by the way. My father always has mottoes and such, and it seemed like a good idea for me to choose one to guide my life too.

Shivering with excitement, I put down the diary to let the words sink in. Alice was writing well over a hundred years ago, but I felt a connection to so much in her entry. 1600 sometimes *did* feel like a jail! My parents were always freaking out about privacy too! And I wasn't totally sure what she meant about "eating up the world," but I liked the sound of that. I murmured those words aloud, then picked the journal back up and turned to the next entry.

October 5, 1901
Diary—

I have been busy, trying to be helpful and watch my little siblings as we slowly settle into our new home.

The first floor is formal and public, where we dine and entertain and the like. The second floor has the seven bedrooms, some sitting rooms, my father's library, and the president's offices, which are separated by glass partitions from the rest of the floor. A musty smell abounds, the floors creak, and paint peels on the second floor, but there is a newly installed elevator. My stepmother has made our room assignments at long last. I came out fairly well. My bedroom is on the northwest side of the floor, next to my sister Ethel's room and catty-corner from my stepmother's sitting room. (Coincidence? Surely not.) It's a large room, though, with lovely windows. I can peer down from them and see Lafayette Square and the grand houses (mansions, really) of John Hay and Henry Adams. Last night I stood in here and watched the view as the sun went down, and the room was full of the most beautiful light. Unfortunately the furniture is not up to par. It's positively Spartan compared to what I have at Sagamore, our house on Oyster Bay, where my room is very fashionable and has nice chintz curtains and a happy floral pattern on the wallpaper. This room has big, cumbersome furniture made of black walnut wood. The pieces are ugly and dull. I have two inferior brass beds—couldn't they have one pleasant *bed instead of two creaky ones? I'll have it redecorated, though. Renovations will start shortly, under the watchful and persnickety command of First Lady Edith Roosevelt. Shockingly, we are in agreement about something: that the private residence is in shambles. I know I'm belaboring the decrepit state of the White House, but it still shocks me how ramshackle it is. It reminds me of Dickens's* Great Expectations *and Miss Havisham's home— both are full of cobwebs and nostalgia gone awry.*

In addition to our tray-sledding, my siblings and I have taken to racing through the upstairs hall on our stilts and bicycles. You wouldn't think, with my crippled history of orthopedic footwear, that I would be any good at stilts. The leg braces I had as a child prevented my feet from turning inward like those of a pigeon. It was a result of polio going undiagnosed. Those darned braces were terribly uncomfortable, and they used to lock up and make me pitch forward, face-first. But the challenges I faced early in life with my legs have only made me strong as a young woman. I practice yoga exercises, which help stretch my limbs, and I am so limber that I can put my leg behind my head. I find it oddly relaxing. It drives Edith mad; she thinks yoga is strange and horribly unladylike.

We and our stilts and bicycles are strictly for-bidden from the first floor…when it is open to the public. Otherwise, we have the run of the house. It's already become the Roosevelt zoo with all the children and the animals. We are keeping some pets in the Conservatory, like our blue macaw, Eli Yale. The cumbersome stodgy furniture is remarkably good for playing hide-and-seek. Although I know I am getting too old for childish games, I can't help but join in from time to time. I believe I've found the secret to eter-nal youth, and it's arrested development. Yesterday, Archie and Ted were hiding behind chairs in the East Room, waiting for visitors to come to see Father so they could pop out and scare them. I couldn't stop laughing, though, and I am afraid my bark kept giving us away.

To Thine Own Self Be True,
Alice

Chapter 4

Footsteps, heavy ones, coming down the hallway interrupted my reading. It didn't sound like my mom's
heels or my dad's loafers, so I knew it was probably a
Secret Service guy doing rounds. No matter who it was,
I *really* didn't want anyone to bother me. I had uncovered
one-hundred-plus-year-old artifacts, *belonging to a famous
person*, hiding under a floorboard. They would get confis-
cated instantly if anyone else found out, and surely sent off
to a museum where historians wearing little white gloves
would pore all over them or keep them under glass. I'd
never get a chance to read it again, at least not like this.
Turning the pages that Alice herself poured her thoughts
onto, in the very rooms in which she wrote. If I believed in
ghosts or spirits, I would think that she was here with me
as I read. That's how strong her personality was, even on
the page. It filled the room.

I knew a bit about girls who lived in 1600 before

me, thanks to a book someone gave me before I moved in. I read it three times and sucked up all the good facts: Caroline Kennedy had a pony named Macaroni, and she let it run all over the grounds. Chelsea Clinton loved dance, like me—but she liked ballet, not jazz. Denise would've *loved* her. Amy Carter had a dog named Grits, and they used to hang out in a treehouse she had on the South Lawn. And Susan Ford got to hold her senior prom in 1600. But those are facts, not feelings. Sometimes I've wondered how other First Kids felt about living here, especially when I'm feeling homesick or annoyed at Denise or nervous about my mom traveling. Was living here always great for them? In that book, Susan Ford said that life at 1600 is "like a fairy tale." Sometimes I wonder if the fairy tale she meant was "Rapunzel," in which a girl gets locked up in a tower for years and has to put her life on hold. It feels most like that to me. I ran my fingertips over the diary in my hands, and breathed in its scent of old leather and paper.

The footsteps came closer, stepping into the pantry next door. I scooped everything up and knotted the handkerchief into a bundle again. I stood and slipped the bundle inside the waistband of my pajama pants, pressing it into my hip with my elbow so it wouldn't slip out as I walked. In my other hand, I held my mug of tea. Then I casually sauntered out of the dining room. The Secret Service guy waved hello from the kitchen doorway as I passed by on my way to my room. "Don't leave on account of me. Just doing rounds."

"No, it's past my bedtime anyway. Night!" I grinned and hustled over to my door. Somebody had shut it after I left, so I struggled to open it, raising my diary-balancing leg to keep the bundle from dropping while I used that hand to open the door. I sloshed some tea on my shirt and the door frame.

"Need help?" The agent looked puzzled by my weird leg position.

"No, I'm stretching. A dance stretch. Eleventh position." I don't think there is an eleventh position, but I doubt he knew his first from fifth. My door finally popped open and I hopped inside. I grabbed the bundle before it could fall to the floor—I was terrified of screwing up anything inside. I looked around my room, thinking that one nice thing about living in 1600 today was that I got free rein to put up *my* posters and *my* pictures in my room—and I picked out all the furniture myself. It was a nicer looking room than my bedroom in St. Paul. And it didn't smell musty at all, thanks to the hardworking cleaning staff. Poor Alice, having to downgrade her bedroom once she moved to the White House. After setting my cold tea on my bedside table, I sat down with the diary and dove back in to Alice's version of 1600.

October 16, 1901
Diary—

Today I miss my Auntie Bye's joyous home in New York City, right at the corner of 62nd and Madison, and the time we shared there. I miss it even though she and her husband, Cowles, now live nearby on N Street and I am often at their home, basking in Bye's extensive and well-appointed library and drinking tea. Today I craved an afternoon tea, but when I went about getting a pot for myself, Stepmother insisted that I take it up to my room. Never mind that my room is a dreadful mess and no place for a proper English-style tea, taken like Bye taught me, with piping hot Earl Grey and plenty of buttery, paper-thin bread. I should have expected that the volume of rules surrounding me would only grow once we took up residence in the White House. I can't stand for them, though. I am positively allergic to discipline. I think I have mentioned that my aim is to eat up the world. Having a decent tea is part of that.

Perhaps the slew of rules are partly because the last time the Roosevelts took Washington by storm, four years ago when Father became Assistant Secretary of the Navy, poor Alice proved to be too much storm for her family to handle. I would spend all day on my bicycle, riding the hills of Washington with my feet up on the handlebars. I broke my curfew more times than I could possibly count. I had my secret club of boys, and we ran riot all over and under and through. Usually I led them in the mischief, the little tomboy hellion that I was. Once I concocted a plan to get my friend Thomas in the house without my parents knowing. I gave him one of my old dresses, some girl's shoes, a hat, and gloves. That evening he came to the door dressed in my cast-offs and tried to gain entry as a girl. He said his name was Estella. It was harmless fun, but the poor thing didn't fool the housekeeper (who recognized the dress she'd laundered for years, of course—I've never had many of them) and then all hell broke loose. Father even called me a guttersnipe (the nerve!), which was a real slap in the face. So the day after my birthday he and Edith shipped me off to Bye's house in New York, despite my pleas to stay. As much as I don't like Father telling me what to do, I hated the idea of the rest of my family together without me—it validated, to me and the rest of the world, the notion that I'm only halfway part of the Roosevelt clan. There was no changing his mind, though, and poor Alice was cast out.

Life at Bye's was wonderful, though. I am certain that if Bye were a man, she would be president and not my father. I have always felt warm and safe and loved in her home, which is hospitable, refined, and always full of great and lively minds. Bye always calls me "Alice" when the rest of my family will not. (To my father I'm never "Alice," but "Sister" and "Sissy." He'll use any nickname to avoid uttering my name, which is also the name of my late mother, Alice Lee.) Bye took me in as an infant, and I know it broke her heart to give me back to my family at the tender age of three. I suppose it broke mine too, but I don't remember it. Every time we've parted since, even for only a few days, I feel a wrenching in my chest. I keep a letter from Bye in my jewel box, which reads "Remember, my blue-eyed darling, if you are very unhappy you can always come back to me." It gives me some comfort when I'm in the storm of a dark mood.

Now I must go, for I hear Eli Yale making a fuss in the Conservatory, and I want to make myself scarce in case the maids complain about his droppings again.

To Thine Own Self Be True,
Alice

I stopped reading for a second to think. Reading Alice's diary *did* feel like talking to someone. *It'll be like having an imaginary older sister.* I'd always wanted one; Harrison was as close as I got. Maybe Alice could be something like my First-Daughter mentor—even if she lived in the olden days so her diary would not be giving me tips on decoding flirty texts or jeans shopping. *Alice seems supercool.* I flipped back to the entry in which she sneaked in her friend, "Estella." I laughed out loud, rereading it. Did Alice really think she could fool someone by making her guy friend wear a dress? Security must have been very different back then. I wonder if the Roosevelt White House had armed Marine sentries as doormen.

Sneaking in Thomas got Alice shipped off to her aunt's house. I've been shipped off too—I spent much of the campaign living at Harrison's. I love him and Max, and their house in Madison is always full of music and delicious food and happiness. Staying with them in Wisconsin wasn't a bad way to live, but it was strange to be away from my parents so much. At least my dad made sure to call me every single night, and sometimes we Skyped while watching our favorite dance-competition show. Dad couldn't help it that the grant meant he had to start up his new lab right away. But sometimes I wondered—why wasn't I as important as the grant? I needed him then, especially as my mom closed in on the presidency.

It was getting late—the White House was as quiet and still as it ever got—but I couldn't put the diary away for the night. I flipped to the next entry.

November 14, 1901
Diary—

At long last I've settled into life as a First Daughter, and I find it quite to my liking. I've reacquainted myself with some old Washingtonian friends. Our gang is called the Gooey Brotherhood of Slimy Slopers, quite a juvenile nonsense name, but I am rather fond of it. We all gather at Bye's for meetings. I'm lucky to have her, for it's very difficult to entertain at the White House. I lack a sitting room, and I am only allowed to entertain in the Green or Red rooms. They are in full view of all of the staff, not to mention my five siblings and parents. It's like throwing a party in a fishbowl. So we go to Bye's refuge and meet in her parlor, where she holds such very intellectual salons for her friends. We Slopers do discuss literature and great ideas, but also try out all the new dances. The other day I taught my friends the hootchy-kootchy, which I first encountered when helping my father open the Buffalo Exposition. There I, totally transfixed, watched a troupe of female dancers swaying their hips in unison, as their arms moved in a serpentine manner above their heads. Edith clucked her tongue next to me, but I studied the scandalous steps and started practicing them in my bedroom when I got back home. I am quite the dancer, bum legs and all.

When I'm back at the White House, so much of my time now is spent with Stepmother making arrangements for my coming-out ball. I am enchanted by the prospect of a White House debut. It will be the most fabulous, glorious debutante ball Washington has ever seen, and loads better than any in New York. There may be many girls richer than I am, but none of them can have their debuts at the residence of the president. Stepmother just today arranged for Belle Hagner, party planner extraordinaire, to help us with all of the arrangements. Now I am about to make a list of all that I must have, so I can present her with a list of my essentials tomorrow. I know I am asking for the moon, but I am the First Daughter so quite frankly I do think that I am entitled to it.

To Thine Own Self Be True,
Alice

November 28, 1901
Diary—

I have an introduction to make to you! I have a new
playmate in the White House. I've recently acquired a
lovely little green garter snake, whom I have christened
"Emily Spinach." Emily in honor of my aunt Emily,
because both are unusually long and thin, like string
beans. Spinach, naturally, because of my dear snake's
bright green color. The endlessly entertaining Emily
Spinach loves to wrap herself around my arm. She
distinguishes me from your average girl, who would
run away in fear of a snake and not wear it around
her neck like a scarf or let its little flicking tongue lick
her elbow gloves. I've had so much fun "introducing"
her to guests of the White House. One visitor was so
shocked and frightened upon seeing me wandering the
White House with Emily looped over my shoulder that
she fainted and had to be revived with smelling salts.
How silly—Emily's just a harmless snake! (You can
imagine my stepmother's reaction.) They tried to make
me get rid of her, but I pitched a fit. I don't see what
the issue is. When I'm not bringing Emily around the
house for socializing, she happily stays in a little stock-
ing box in my room. It's not as though I let her slither

free through the East Room or the dining areas. Well, sometimes I do bring her around to parties, but I keep her tucked in my purse.

Although my father disapproves of how I am "deliberately trying to shock with that little snake," nobody is more of a champion of wildlife than him. Thanks to that, I know that there is little risk of me being forced to dispose of Emily Spinach. My father will even play with her too, on the rare occasions that he is home and not working. Then he'll go on wild tangents and tell me tales of buffaloes and bears and elk and the other beasts he's encountered out west. One day I wandered into his office with Emily on my arm as he was meeting with his journalist friend Mr. Wister. Mr. Wister was quite taken aback by my little snake and me, but my father simply said, "I can either run the country or I can control Alice, but I can't possibly do both." Emily and I laughed. Father picks his battles well.

To Thine Own Self Be True,
Alice

Chapter 5

R eading Alice's weird, old-timey cursive was a challenge, so I only made it through two more entries before I decided to stop for the night. *Alice was incredible. How come I haven't heard more about her before this?* The book I'd read on First Kids never talked about Alice, but I guess that's because it started with the Kennedys. I slid from my bedspread to my rug, where the handkerchief, cigarettes, and postcards were strewn, to examine the pictures again. One more time, I reread the entry about sliding down the stairways on tray tables from the kitchen. *Inauguration of Fun.* Picturing that scene made me giggle. 1600 probably *would* be more fun if I had siblings, like Alice had, or at least some cousins. My whole life I've felt cheated that I'm an only child. There has never been a kid table at Calloway/Rhodes family holiday meals because I'm the only kid in the clan. Period. Harrison tried to make me feel better once by saying, "It's okay—your dad and I are immature anyway. Remember this, Audrey:

You're only young once, but you can be immature forever."
Reminds me of Alice's comment about eternal youth and
arrested development.

It was almost midnight, but I was too wired to sleep. I
opened the door to my room slowly. *Maybe I don't need to
feel like a prisoner in my room. Alice certainly didn't.* I strolled
through the quiet, dark halls, triggering on lights wherever I
went—1600 has motion sensors to turn off lights in unused
rooms as part of its green initiative. I passed a guard or two
as I made my way to the lower level, waving and hurrying
ahead before they could ask me where I was going. I bet they
thought it was a midnight cookie run.

I skipped the halls as I headed downstairs, crossing my
fingers that the door to the bowling alley wasn't locked. It
wasn't, so I walked in and plopped down on the floor to
unlace my sneakers. "This is my version of tray sledding, I
guess," I muttered. The pins were all lined up at the far end
of the lane, as if they'd been waiting for me to wander in to
play. I grabbed a ball and sent it rumbling toward the pins. I
slid around on the waxed wood floor in my socks, watching
as the ball inched down the lane. Gutter ball.

"I'm just warming up!" I called to the empty room. I
threw another ball and managed to hit three. I slid down the
lane to the pins and reset them (if the lane had an automatic
resetting thing like Elsie's Bowling back home, it wasn't

turned on). Some security guy was probably watching me via closed-circuit TV somewhere, laughing hysterically. I craned my neck to look around for a security camera. Not finding one, I twirled around, waving at all corners. I danced around in what I felt the hootchy-kootchy should be as I made my way back to the start of the lane. "This one's for you, overnight-shift guard!" I took a running start and lobbed another ball down the lane. It struck five pins with a satisfying *thwack*. "Sweet!" I jumped up and thrust my fist in the air. I dedicated my next attempt to Nixon, since he was the president who put in a bowling alley.

I kept bowling until my right arm and wrist ached. I plopped down in the middle of the single lane and stretched out, staring at the ceiling. I checked my watch, and it was almost two in the morning. I reset the pins one last time, because I felt bad leaving the alley in disarray for the cleaning people.

I headed up to the third floor, to the game room. I flipped on the lights and walked over to the foosball table, figuring out pretty quickly that it's awfully hard to play foosball alone. I spun the knob on one side and tried running over to the opposite, but all I succeeded in was jabbing myself in the ribs with a handle. I decided to pass on table hockey. Disappointed, I left and walked into the Solarium. I approached the outside door, wanting to step out on the

Promenade and take in the Washington night sky. But I wasn't allowed to go out there at night, and I'd started to get sleepy. Skipping back to my room, I thought it wasn't quite racing stilts and bicycles through the first floor, but Alice would've approved if she could've seen me having fun tonight. If I wasn't eating up the world at least I was nibbling it.

After breakfast the next morning, I settled in the Solarium with the journal, my laptop, and a fresh thermos of tea. I started researching Teddy Roosevelt online. He was the twenty-sixth president, known for something called progressive reform and conservation. And teddy bears were named after him. Alice was his oldest daughter, a wild child who moved into the White House as a teenager. That surprised me—given the way Alice talked and her stunts like tray-sliding and pet-snake wrangling, she seemed a little younger. But, she was living in a different era. *Or maybe Alice was on to something?* Maybe when you find yourself cooped up in "the crown jewel of the Federal prison system," as President Truman had called it (Harrison told me that in an email), the only way to stay sane and entertained is by being a little crazy. Eccentric. Alice's life in the White House didn't sound boring at all so far, unlike mine.

I went online to start researching more about Alice's life, but my fingers froze in midair as I was about to type in her name. *What will the fun be of reading Alice's diary if I already know what happened to her?* That would spoil all the secrets, and Alice already seemed like the kind of girl who'd have loads of juicy secrets. I decided right then that I wasn't going to do any more Alice research—at least not until I'd read the whole journal.

I shut my laptop. I was *dying* to know what happened with Alice's big debutante ball thingy. Did she get everything she wanted? I picked up the journal to find out firsthand.

December 13, 1901
Diary—

I took a break from the debut planning today for a lengthy pillow fight with my siblings. Kermit started it, whacking Ethel with a heavy down pillow as she came out of her bedroom. Those two tend to be at each other's throats. Soon we were all in the fray, winding up in the attic wing with feathers raining down on us. When the fat pillows had turned thin, Ethel suggested that we settle scores by racing stilts and bicycles. I beat them all on my trusty stilts. I had a leg up, literally, because of my years with those braces.

It felt strange to wander down to the first floor after those activities and make debut arrangements.

Of course I am excited to enter society. Yet it's tinged bittersweet, especially for me as the oldest in the family. I certainly hope a debuted young lady can still partake in an attic pillow fight, now and then. Then again, when have I ever concerned myself with the rules?

I was still flushed, with my hair falling out of my bun, and Belle Hagner asked if I intended to appear like such a "ragamuffin" in society. I rolled my eyes until Edith reprimanded me for my attitude. She and I have been battling about the specific plans for my party. Despite being the child of a World Leader, Rough Rider, Master of the Bully Pulpit, I shall not get everything I want. For example: the dance floor. I was told that I had to seek the approval of Congress to get the renovations necessary to make the White House ballroom presentable. I cornered a few congressmen and gave them my very best Auntie Corinne "elbow-in-the-soup" treatment—feigning interest in every boring detail that they told me about their legislation, nodding and blinking my big blue eyes and exclaiming, "Oh! How absolutely fascinating!" and "Aren't you just the cleverest chap," at every chance. (Auntie Corinne was and is the master of faking enthusiasm in otherwise dull social settings. She leans in so close to whomever she is speaking to that her elbow tends to be precariously positioned next to, and almost in, her soup bowl. Hence the term "elbow-in-the-soup" treatment.) Perhaps that sly fox Corinne could have won where I lost, but sadly no money came through for poor Alice's ball, and we will be having a slapdash linen-crash floor because the ballroom is without a hardwood floor. I find this personally humiliating.

Then there is the issue of refreshments. I begged and pleaded with Stepmother for champagne, which is the drink in fashion. All the girls having their debuts in New York City are serving it. But apparently those stuffy Women's Christian Temperance Union biddies would drown in disapproval, so we will be serving punch. If they only knew that I have taken to smuggling bottles of whiskey (which I sneak out of the White House stock) into boring dinner parties at teetotaling houses—I hide them in my elbow-length gloves. It's a great way to garner the attention of my male dinner companions, who are always so very grateful for a surreptitious sip.

My gown makes me excited, though. It's achingly beautiful: made of pure white taffeta, with a white chiffon overskirt. The bodice is appliquéd with tiny white rosebuds, scores and scores of them embracing my torso. I have a very elegant, very simple diamond *pendant necklace. When the light catches it, it takes my breath away. (I will have to stash smelling salts in my elbow gloves, instead of a flask, for that reason.) After the alterations finally were finished, I sneaked the dress up to my room and put it on. Standing in front of my mirror, I got chills. For the first time in ages I didn't see a homely little tomboy, a knock-kneed girl who spent years of her life in ugly metal braces, but a slender young woman. I looked beautiful, and whether I actually am or it's simply the magic of this lovely, breathtaking dress—I don't care. I will always know what I looked like in the mirror right then.*

To Thine Own Self Be True,

Alice

January 4, 1902
Diary—

It's past noon, and I am still lying in my bed (although, as my father likes to comment, I rarely make any appearances before noon these days), reliving last night again and again in my memories. Diary, it was wonderful—every single shining moment. I have so much to write down now because I want to remember the night of my debut for the rest of my life.

The receiving line began at ten o'clock in the Blue Room. And do you know how many people my parents and I received? Over six hundred! I might not have gotten a shiny new hardwood floor, but the decorations almost made up for that. We transformed the Blue Room into something like the hanging gardens of Babylon. Over two thousand flowers covered the room—roses, carnations, hyacinths, narcissus—and there was holly on every lintel. It was thrilling to walk in and see the room decorated beyond my wildest expectations. My gown made me look as lovely as when I tried it on before, which made it easy for me to be confident and proud and charming in front of so very many people. My hair was even done up so as to hide my gargantuan high forehead.

The first waltz played at eleven, and of course it was the U.S. Marine Band playing for me. (No "poor Alice" on that account.) I danced with the positively dashing Lieutenant Gilmore of the Artillery. I was nervous and sure that my gimpy legs would make me trip all over him, but he told me that I was "graceful as a swan." At which of course I had to snicker. It is quite a heady experience dancing at these events—the rooms get warm, and after a few rounds, the gentlemen tend to smell…not so gentle. It can get a little overpowering, especially when you are clutched tightly in a partner's arms, and at times I couldn't tell if I was getting dizzy from all the twirling or from the strong scent of sweat.

After we danced, the buffet started. The only word for it is sumptuous. Finger sandwiches, oysters, aspics and jellies, escargots à bourguignonne, chicken fricassee, roasted beef, savory soups and consommé, puddings, crepes, éclairs, meringues, soufflé, petits fours, and ice cream! No champagne, though, for poor Alice. Just punch. That wish did not come true, and champagne can't easily be smuggled in elbow gloves.

It's silly how these things are set up—first you attack the buffet as though you were a Rough Rider in Cuba at a chuck wagon, then you find a gent and dance or stroll the promenade. More like roll the promenade, after all that food. But my sateen-and-whalebone health corset did not permit me to sample as much as I desired of the delicious spread. One of the dear kitchen maids put aside some goodies for me in the icebox, so whenever I finally drag myself from this bed I can start sampling what my guests enjoyed.

I don't much care for public speaking—actually I don't care for it at all; it makes me frightened and faint.

The kind of attention I got last night, though, I adore. All those eyes on me in my gorgeous dress, specifically the male eyes. Many handsome lads attended last night, and I flirted like mad with them. Auntie Corinne remarked to me that there was a crowd "seven-men deep" around me, the whole night. I don't know if that is precisely true, but I did have a lot of admirers. I suppose because it was my fancy party and I was wearing an ethereal dress. There wouldn't be a crowd for me as I look this morning, puffy-faced and tired and entirely without fuss and finery. Don't think I'm playing "poor Alice," though. It was a lovely, fantastic evening, and I felt the same: lovely and fantastic. Filled to the brim with happiness.

Now my stomach is growling in a very unladylike way (I am a lady now, I suppose—how strange) so I am off to raid the icebox.

To Thine Own Self Be True,
Alice

January 5, 1902
Diary—

All of those good feelings from yesterday have evaporated. Poof! The papers chimed in on my debut (some even on the front page!), and they've offered faint praise. First off with the little good: The New York Tribune did say, "A more charming debutante has rarely been introduced in Washington." They went on to tell that I was "attractive in my dignified simplicity and natural grace as I was beautiful. Tall, with a striking figure, blue eyes, and a fine fair complexion, she was certainly one of the prettiest girls in Washington." One of the prettiest girls in Washington! My cousin Eleanor will die when she reads that. Of course, that wasn't so much my figure as it was that of my undergarments, but I won't quibble.

Unfortunately, the New York Times called my decorations "extremely simple." I am livid. How could anyone enter the Blue Room and say that about it? Of all the people reported to have "simple" decorations—the girl in the White House should not. It's perplexing, but one of the papers actually raved about the linen-crash floor, saying that dancing on it was a delight. I would suggest that the reviewer had imbibed a little too much champagne, but I was not allowed to serve any. (I will quit lamenting that now, I swear on the Sloper handbook.)

According to Stepmother, today's papers still buzzed about me, despite those lukewarm assessments.

"Princess Alice" is what the reporters are starting to call me, and the readers are clamoring for more details about me. It is peculiar, isn't it? Interest in my father is understandable because of who he is and what he has done. But I am simply a girl whose father is a politician. If you ask me, there's comparatively little special about Alice. I suppose once all the details of my debut have been discussed ad nauseam the interest will wane.

Now I have little to occupy myself with here. Partly I hoped that some gent and I would experience love at first sight at my ball (I was dressed appropriately for a run-in with Cupid's arrow, certainly) and now I could throw myself into writing torrid love letters and planning clandestine meetings on the South Lawn or the stables. It might sound contrary, but a beau-turned-husband is a ticket to get out of my father's house and into the world on my own. Ironic as it may be, marrying may be my best shot at freedom. 'Tis a pity, but none of the boys at the ball made much of an impression on me. Lacking anything else to fill my time with, I suppose I'll return to learning Greek.

To Thine Own Self Be True,
Alice

Chapter 6

Someone knocking on the Solarium door interrupted my reading. It was the social secretary's assistant, wondering if she could please interrupt me for a minute to discuss dinner attire. *Crap!* I'd forgotten about dinner with the German chancellor. Maybe part of me wanted to forget—State Dinners are definitely not my preferred way to spend a weekend night. They used to make me nervous, but now they just annoy me. Other than saying hello to whichever head of state we're meeting, I don't say a word. For *hours*. It's like olden times, when kids were seen and not heard, which is so boring. Amy Carter used to bring a book to the table. I tried that once, but Denise snatched it away.

I gently slid Alice's diary under a newspaper, then watched as the assistant held up a few truly stupid-looking dresses for me to choose from. It's like the East Wing people have so little faith in my ability to act normal that every little detail, down to my shoes, has to be micromanaged. *Did I ever do a single thing wrong during the entire campaign? Or my mom's long career in the Senate? Nope.* I fantasized about strolling down in my favorite holey jeans and some Keds, just to see their reactions. Or a stunning grown-up dress, like Alice's debut gown. All the choices I'm given are old-fashioned and/or babyish, thanks to Bikinigate.

Last summer my mom and I were scheduled to travel around the world, while my dad stayed home to run his experiments. Our fantastic itinerary—Majorca, Rome, Prague, Kiev, Moscow, Hong Kong, Taipei, Vancouver, then to our house in St. Paul for two weeks, and finally back to DC—was interrupted when paparazzi ambushed us on the beach in Spain. The tabloids back home went wild. *Madam Presi-DON'T* blared the headlines, with pictures of my mom in a Lands' End tankini on Alcudia beach. (Can you imagine how awful that would be? Your *mom* in her *swimsuit* on the cover of every paper? Seriously.) I turned on the satellite TV in Air Force One at night and, to my horror, heard a comedian on some late-night talk show make squicky jokes about my mom's cleavage. The horror.

One magazine ran a two-page spread with shots of me in my totally modest two-piece. The White House felt compelled to issue a statement about the inappropriateness of publishing the photos, and the whole thing mushroomed into "Bikinigate." First the editorials questioned, *Is it appropriate for the president to be in public in swimwear?* Then cable-news anchors gravely stated, *Parents around the country are asking: Is it acceptable for a thirteen-year-old to wear a bikini?* and *Should the First Family be allowed the privacy of a "normal" vacation, without photographers and the press?* My mom's political opponents made snide comments like, *Why is the president traipsing around with her daughter in the midst of a budget crisis?* All this because we wore swimsuits at a beach. We never made it past Rome, and I spent the rest of the summer hiding out in DC, except for the promised two weeks back in St. Paul. Ever since, my clothing options have been limited and vaguely Amish.

"Those are my only choices?" I asked the assistant. "Nothing a little more...mature?"

The assistant shook her head, her arms sinking from holding up the hangers so long. "These are all I have to offer." I rolled my eyes and picked the dress in her left hand, muttering my disapproval. It was cut almost like a jumper and had kiddish pockets, but at least it was black. The other one had pink daisies all over it. "I'll have it pressed and in your room by four," the assistant said. I heard her heels clacking down the hall behind her as she left. I love the noise heels make. Mom's staffers always make me wear Mary Janes for events. Not even ballet flats—and I'm a dancer.

I slouched in my chair and stared out the window. Alice had no idea how lucky she was, throwing a party like that. Wearing a beautiful dress, one that transformed her from gawky to elegant. I closed my eyes and imagined sweeping into tonight's dinner in a stunning floor-length gown. Which would look insane, because this wasn't a fancy dinner, just a formal one. I revised my fantasy to me walking in looking drop-dead gorgeous. Grown-up, in makeup and heels. (I included a cute German son of the chancellor in this version.)

Eventually I got up and went downstairs. The dress was hanging on a hook next to my closet, perfectly pressed. Polished Mary Janes sat next to my closet door. I sighed and walked over to put the dress on, but before I could pull it off the hanger, my mom barged into my room. She used to drop her capital-*P* Politician mannerisms with her briefcase at the door, but at some point in the past several years she started carrying on with them at home, walking as stiffly and briskly into rooms as when she's on Capitol Hill. It's weird.

"Hey! What about knocking?"

"Sorry, Audrey." My mother sat down on the bed, gingerly, like she still wasn't used to being in this unfamiliar yellow room. "What are you up to?" It was the first time I'd seen her since Thursday, but I didn't feel like updating her on my life. *You snooze, you lose.*

72

"Nothing." I pulled off my hoodie and casually threw it over the Alice paraphernalia on my floor. My mom has eagle eyes, and I didn't want to share that stuff. At least, not yet.

She smiled. "I'm glad to see that you're treating your room exactly like you do at home. It looks like a clothes bomb went off in here."

I raised an eyebrow. "Can we say the *b*-word in here?" She laughed, and I sat down next to her. "Are you here to talk clothes for tonight? I already picked out something appropriately dorky with one of the assistants."

My mom tipped her head down and smiled. "You caught me. Although I wanted to sit and chat with my lovely daughter for a minute too."

Her earnestness made me squirm. I used to love it when we'd catch up in my room back home or crawl into one of the hotel beds after a long day on the campaign trail that summer before the election. We'd talk about the places she'd delivered her stump speech at—laughing at how many local delicacies (like gut-busting chili dogs) we had to shove down our throats, or the baby that spit up on her when she was leaning in for a cliché kiss. Mom was as busy then as now, but it was different. We still had watched TV while eating room service together. When school made it impossible for me to travel around with her, she had made a point to come home for one long weekend a month. We got real breaks from the election stuff and politics. But the president rarely gets breaks, and my mom was almost never home for a full twenty-four hours anymore. I feel guilty admitting this, because I know the pressures on her, but it made me angry.

Mom smiled at me again. "Tell me all about your week, honey." I opened my mouth as she glanced away. An aide lurked in the open doorway. "On second thought, I think I'm being summoned. Come downstairs by six-thirty, okay? We'll catch up later."

"Sure, Mom." She strode back out the door, plucking a memo from the aide's hand before she even started down the hall. I was left staring at the fugly jumper dress next to my closet. *Yuck. Alice would not be caught dead in a dress like that.* (Aside from the fact that it would show her ankles, and Alice probably would be into that taboo.) She wore clothes that made her feel beautiful and grown-up. *I am sick of wearing a little girl's clothes, especially in public.* It was too late for me to try the elbow-in-the-soup treatment on the assistant who picked out my outfit, and my mom was obviously too busy to talk, so I would have to make a wardrobe adjustment without consulting them.

The jumper found its way to a pile of clothes on my floor and I found my way into the dress from my flapper costume. It's not a costumey dress—it's the real thing. Vintage, emerald green, fringed, and swingy. Maybe a little bit low-cut (Mom made me wear a leotard under it before), and it stops a couple inches from my knees. The dress looks amazing on me, though. I wore it when my dance company in St. Paul commissioned new choreography to *Rhapsody in Blue*, when I had my first solo. I danced around in front of my mirror, listening to the swish of the fringe. It tickled my bare legs. I skipped the leotard. To thine own self be true, right?

I sneaked into my mom's dressing room and hit up her shoes. I'm almost a half-size larger than her, but I can squeeze into some of her pairs. I found a pair of extra-fancy black heels—tall, with red paint on the bottom. *Excellent.* Then I wandered over to her vanity and started messing around with her makeup. I didn't put a lot on—just a few swipes of mascara and some red lipstick. I stood in front of her big mirror and did a twirl. I looked amazing: not at all like a little girl, and I loved it. Like Alice, I was transformed. I couldn't wait to see how people would react to the new me.

A little after 6:30 p.m.—I wanted to make a dramatic entrance—I headed down to the Diplomatic Reception Room, where we always meet important State guests. I tottered a little wherever I hit thick carpet. *How the heck do women walk around in these things all day long?* Walking the long halls took forever, but finally I click-clacked my way into the room. My parents, some aides and the Chief

75

of Staff, one of the official White House photographers, and the Germans—Chancellor Klaus Bergermann; his wife, Margaret; some of their aides; and who I assumed to be Bergermann's teenage daughter—were already standing around, taking pictures.

I stopped in the doorway, one hand on my hip. My shoulders were thrown back in my best, most confident posture. I raised my chin and smiled broadly.

"Audrey, dear, come in—" my mother started, then her eyes broke from mine and scanned down my body, stopping at her tall, tall shoes. Mom's mouth hung open. "Audrey?"

"Yes?" I kept grinning, but I noticed how quiet everything had gotten. There's usually a constant murmur in the White House, but I could hear only my pulse pounding inside my head.

The assistant from this morning appeared at my side. "*What are you wearing?*" she hissed in my ear. I felt my cheeks start burning, even though the room felt cold and disapproving. This was not exactly what I had expected. *I only wanted people to see me as I am, or want to be—not some silent, boring little girl.*

Finally, someone broke the silence. "I adore your dress," the teenage girl said with a strong German accent, walking forward. The rest of the room watched as she came to my side. "I am impressed by your shoes too."

My mother turned and tried to smile at the other guests. "Audrey, meet Heidi Bergermann." But Mom was fighting a grimace, so the corners of her mouth kept turning down. It looked like her face was half-paralyzed. "Please excuse me, I seem to have stalled in our introductions. I was taken by surprise by your lovely…gown." I cringed, but everyone else laughed good-naturedly and stopped staring at me, turning back to the conversations they'd been immersed in before I entered the room—although a few curious guests kept glancing back at me, and at least one person took my picture. I planted myself next to Heidi, hoping that my parents would not come over to freak out on me if I stayed next to the chancellor's kid. *What was I thinking? Maybe someone like Alice Roosevelt could stun a room with a beautiful dress, but not me.* I sighed.

The girl, Heidi, leaned in to talk to me. "These things can be difficult, no? Sometimes you just want to…do something unexpected." She squeezed my arm reassuringly. "At least, I do." Then Heidi pushed her thick, long red hair behind one ear, showing me a glimpse of a tattoo covering the side of her neck. It looked so strange on an otherwise conservatively dressed, fresh-faced girl. I couldn't tell if it was real or temporary. "I think wearing your cool dress to dinner is, how do you say, *inspired.*"

I grinned and was about to tell Heidi how happy I was

that she understood when my mother appeared by my side. "Excuse me. May I have a moment with my daughter?" Mom was smiling but had the same icy look in her eyes that she got when an opponent told her to "man up" during a debate—peeved, but trying to hide it.

"Certainly, Madam President. Audrey, it was very nice to meet you." I nodded. A lump was forming in my throat. *Mom is going to kill me now. At least there will be witnesses.* I reluctantly followed her out into the hall, where a few staffers were waiting.

"We will discuss this *in depth* later," she said quietly, "but for now, put this on." An aide stepped forward and handed me a black shawl. "And wipe off that makeup." I nodded and wobbled off to the bathroom to wash my face. Even though my mom was clearly mad, I didn't feel particularly bad. Actually, I felt frustrated right back at her.

The rest of the dinner was fine, although I was barefaced and swathed in a massive pashmina that hid most of my dress. All I could concentrate on during the event was how much the shawl made my skin itch.

Around eleven, the knock I'd been dreading came on my door. "Come in," I called and slouched into my pillows, pulling up the covers. Maybe if they saw me in bed they'd keep the lecturing short. Both of my parents walked in, still in formal attire.

"Audrey," my mom started, "wardrobe for dinners with heads of state is *absolutely* nonnegotiable. Period. Thank goodness the chancellor has a teenage daughter himself—he found it amusing that you wore a dance costume. Not all guests would react the same way. What if he thought you weren't taking his visit seriously? Or that you didn't respect him and his office?" I nodded. I hadn't thought about offending someone—whoops.

"Come on, Audrey," my dad added. "You're old enough that you should've known not to wear that." I suppressed the urge to roll my eyes. How could you *not* want to roll your eyes whenever a parent invoked the whole "you're old enough" thing?

"I wasn't wearing a costume, though. I mean, it was part of my dance costume, but it's a dress," I explained. "A grown-up one. For once, I didn't want to look like a little kid. The wardrobe people never listen to me about that."

"Then you should've told me that earlier today, or the assistant who chose your outfit." My mom spoke in the kind of tone that meant she was trying not to blow up but might not succeed.

"Fine. I guess I'll consider my clothes one less thing I get say-so over in this house." I crossed my arms and flopped back into my pillows.

"Audrey. That's not fair," my dad started.

I shot back up. "It's true. Admit it. I am just a prop to be dressed up around here."

My parents glanced at each other. My mother was biting her lip, and my dad whispered something to her. Then he winked at me.

Mom uncrossed her arms. "I don't appreciate your tone. But maybe we should set up a personal shopping session for you next week so you can get some new options."

I refused to smile but did stop furrowing my eyebrows. "Good. I mean, thanks." I felt a teensy bit less pissed at her. "Sorry if I embarrassed you."

"Apology accepted," my mother said, uncrossing her arms. "Now it's time for bed." My parents came over to give me very perfunctory kisses good night and then left the room. I stretched across my bed and stared up at the veiny ceiling, smiling. At the next State Dinner, maybe I'd have my own pair of heels. *Perhaps tonight hasn't been such a disaster after all.*

January 30, 1902
Diary—

Interest in me hasn't waned since my debut. People

in this country have gone absolutely crazy for their "Princess Alice!" I've received hundreds of requests for my autograph—enough that White House staff now needs to open my mail for me. Photographers and reporters pursue me whenever I leave the house, and on many occasions small crowds have formed when I am out in public. There still isn't much automobile or carriage traffic when I cruise on my bicycle to Dupont, but there are people who point and exclaim. One morning I awoke to my stepmother all atwitter— some camera fiends were planted at the front door, hoping to get my picture. They weren't even reporters but "fans."

It gets even more peculiar. The most popular songs right now were composed with me as the subject: "The Alice Roosevelt March" and "The American Girl." Probably my favorite homage to moi is the fabric color taking America by storm: "Alice blue," the precise blue-gray color of my eyes—supposedly. No dressmaker has verified it against my peepers. One of the maids told me stores are selling out of it; the papers reported it's the most popular shade for dresses right now. (How lucky for the ladies of America that my eyes aren't a muddy brown.) My photograph decorates tinted postcards and fancy French chocolate cards. *It's wild. As one of my Sloper friends remarked, perhaps with a smidgen of jealousy, the world has become my oyster. If I had anything to be vain about, I suppose I would be getting very vain. Luckily for the world at large, my gargantuan forehead (among other attributes) prevents me from that sin.*

My parents do not think it is so "wild." My step-mother's constant refrain: "Beware of publicity!" "Do not talk to reporters!" She says nice girls do not get their pictures in the paper, much less on chocolate cards, except for when they are born, married, and buried. I say pop-pycock to that. Actually, I asked Edith whether she'd like to find me a husband then, or otherwise put some arsenic in my tea because I've already been born. My father had the audacity to accuse me of courting publicity. Of all the people to say such a thing—my father, who has to be the bride at every wedding, the baby at every christening, and the corpse at every funeral. He never met a form of public attention that he didn't love. Why, at the inaugu-ration, I remember him chiding me for waving gleefully to some friends in the audience while he spoke. I said, "Why shouldn't I?" "But this is my inauguration!" was his exasperated reply. For him, the master of publicity, to criticize me for having a little fun with the attention—it's hypocrisy, pure and simple.

So I am told I must never, ever, ever, ever speak to reporters and should avoid photographers at all times. Cover my face if I have to. And yet, there is interest in every move my family or I make! How absurd. My siblings share my bemusement—Ted even sent me a letter from school with a postscript reading "Five cents for the signature please." I nearly died laughing. (I suppose Edith would've allowed my name to appear in the paper then.)

But try telling any of this to my parents, with their fuss-box ideas of how young ladies should behave. Things are rather strained between my father and me lately. There's no distinction between when he is working and when he is in his home anymore. Even that handy glass partition between his offices and our residence doesn't separate the two for him. I miss the time he used to have for us—did you know I used to demand that he carry me downstairs to breakfast every morning via a piggyback ride? I would stand at my doorway and bellow, "Now, pig!" and off we'd go. I'd sit in on his morning shave too, and in between swipes with the razor, he'd tell me tales of the wilderness out west. But he'd never tell me any stories related to my mother. He hasn't spoken of her, to anyone, since the day she died. Bye told me once my father's peculiar

silence is because he feels such terrible guilt for remar-
rying. I suspect I must bring out that guilt in him too.

So you can see that even before all the country
wanted a piece of Alice, things between my parents and
me were rocky. If anything, that discord spurs me to
pursue what I want even more, and right now what I
want is to eat up this attention with my silver spoon.
And so I shall.

To Thine Own Self Be True,
Alice
P.S. One dollar for the signature please!!!

February 5, 1902
Diary—

Today I shan't be writing of any of the foolish, selfish,
or girlish things that normally fill my silly mind. For
once all my attention is not on the needs and wants of
"poor Alice" (do take notice). My darling brother Ted,
my boon companion, is gravely sick. Off at school, he
has taken ill with pneumonia. Father and Stepmother
assure me that he will overcome it ("Ted's a Tough,
Alice. He'll pull through this."), but fear has stricken
my heart. Perhaps I am prone to fearing that I will

lose those whom I love—remember I never had the chance to know my sweet mother. I couldn't bear it if anything were to happen to my dear brother. The Roosevelt children are split into neat little pairs: Ethel has Kermit, and the little ones Archie and Quentin have each other. Who will I have if I lose Ted? I am absolutely sick with worry and fear.

When Archie had the measles and was confined to his room, Quentin begged a coachman in the White House to help him bring our beloved family pony, Algonquin, up in the elevator. Quentin knew that nothing would cause Archie to rally like a little quality time spent with his trusty steed. And he was right— from the minute tiny Quentin led Algonquin by the reins into his room, Archie was on the mend. Edith was livid when she discovered that there was not only a pony but a few road apples in her invalid son's room.

I want to do something similar for Ted—be the force that helps him heal. I begged Father to let me visit, but he refused. He said that Ted needs time to rest now and having visitors will only tire him. I will keep begging my father until I wear him into the ground. Perhaps, if no other option becomes available to me, I will steal Algonquin to get there.

—Alice

February 26, 1902

Diary—

First—Ted is fine and well now. My parents finally let me go to him. While he recuperated, he had great fun playing with Emily (whom I smuggled in my luggage) and me. We terrorized the poor nurses with Miss Spinach, slipping her in his soup bowl when they'd come to pick up his tray. We sent more dishes clattering to the floor than I could count.

Now—the past three days have been an absolute dream! Yours truly got the honor of christening the Kaiser's yacht. Can you imagine? The German Kaiser himself didn't come to America for his new purchase, but dashing Prince Henry did. He arrived in Washington on the twenty-third. I didn't see him then because I was far too busy preparing for my official duties, i.e., smashing wine bottle after bottle in Auntie Bye's backyard. You see, due to my international popularity those planning the visit decided that I should be the one to crack a bottle of fine champagne against the side of the Meteor as part of the official yacht-christening ceremony. (What a waste of the champagne.) I was terribly nervous about the whole event! I certainly didn't know what amount of force would be necessary to break the darned bottle. But an hour in Bye's backyard and a thorough drenching in sparkling wine left me much more confident about the whole affair.

On the day of the christening we rose early, almost before first light, so we (Father, Stepmother, and myself) would be in Jersey City promptly at seven. I doubt I could have slept later, I was so nervous about my performance. We ate breakfast whilst traveling, and I managed to lap up some tea and toast despite a jittery stomach.

By half-past ten we arrived at the grand boat. I nervously made my way to the yacht, praying that I would remember exactly what I needed to say. "In the name of his Majesty the German Emperor I christen this yacht Meteor." There, I still remember it, and I did then too, speaking clearly and confidently and with a great smile. Next I took an ornamental knife and sliced the last bit of rope that kept it tethered. Edith held her breath beside me, afraid I'd slice my hands. Finally, with a great flourish, I smashed that bottle of fine champagne smack on the bow, sending a joyous spray of bubbly onto the yacht and the cheering onlookers. My parents said that I did a fabulous job and I believe them. Prince Henry made a point of *congratulating me right in front of Edith. Euphoric, I felt as though I'd nipped at Bye's liquor cabinet. But I swear on Ted I hadn't.*

After the formal ceremony we went to the Hohenzollern, the emperor's other yacht, and had a celebratory lunch. I sat next to Prince Henry, on his left, and had bully fun speaking with him. I didn't even have to do Auntie Corinne's elbow-in-the-soup treatment to hold his attention. Contrary to popular belief, not all princes are handsome—but Henry fit the dashing role. Before you get any ideas, Henry is much older than I and happily wed. Anyway, he took one of the lunch cards and drew a charming picture of his favorite stallion for me on it, signing it with his name. On behalf of the emperor, Prince Henry also gave me a beautiful diamond bracelet. He even fastened it to my dainty wrist himself, and I thought my stepmother would have to pull out the smelling salts. All of the fetching officers of the boat presented me with flowers as well. Even though the event intended to honor Prince Henry and the Kaiser, it sure felt as though everyone was honoring Princess Alice.

The newspapers unanimously proclaimed that I did a tremendous job with my official duties. The New York Tribune said that I "seemed unaffected" by all the attention lavished on me (ha-ha) and that I "stood in the glare of the footlights without flinching." As should a Roosevelt! The sole group unhappy with me is the WCTU. Can you believe that those dry nincompoops lobbied for me to use a nonalcoholic substitute for the champagne? You'd think the old biddies would be happy that all the drink went to waste.

I am so proud that for once I could do something publicly that was a boon to my father's presidency. Not that all of the attention I get for my debut or my social events is necessarily bad for him—despite what my stepmother thinks. It is, though, a distraction from whatever real work he does. I am pleased that I could be of diplomatic service. I also hope that now that I've proven what a charming asset I can be, this will be just the start of Alice's political endeavors.

> To Thine Own Self Be True,
> Alice

Chapter 7

I did not get diamond bracelets or champagne toasts out of our dinner with the German chancellor, but I did get a shopping trip with some staffers the next week. I picked out some new, oh-so-slightly more age-appropriate clothes and shoes, although my mom made it clear that she had veto power, especially concerning V-necks. One of the dresses I picked out was blue-gray, and I liked imagining that it was the exact shade of Alice blue. Wednesday I was excited to wear my new pair of yellow flats to school—shoes, I've found, are one of the few ways to express your style in a school with uniforms. I sat down to eat lunch in the cafeteria courtyard, hoping that someone might notice my supercute shoes and maybe that would lead to a conversation. Back in Minnesota, my friends and I were always borrowing each other's clothes and showing off new purchases. But my shoes didn't get any compliments, and I sat alone, eating my sandwich and doing homework.

As I flipped through my history textbook a different classical music motif, this one by Bach, interrupted me. Bach means a special announcement. The PA crackled, "Attention, students. There will be no seventh period today. Instead, there will be an assembly in Friendship Hall. Please report there promptly after sixth period." My sixth period was music history, the one class I shared with Quint. Collectively, the two hundred and seventy-five minutes I spent in that sunny corner room on the top floor of the Upper School building were the best of my week, hands-down, because I had Quint to talk to and I loved listening to music. The music teacher, Mr. Morgan, plays really eclectic stuff for us—everything from ancient chants to Herbie Hancock to Plácido Domingo to The Killers. When I shut my eyes and listen to music, I can be anywhere I want in the world. The day Mr. Morgan played The Beatles' "Here Comes the Sun," I was instantly transported back to the dusty sunroom at Kim's house, dancing around with my best friend. We were obsessed with that song in sixth grade. Hearing anything Tchaikovsky makes me think about Harrison taking me to The Nutcracker ballet every December. Thankfully, Mr. Morgan never played any of the three songs that always blasted out of the speakers before one of my mom's campaign events. After months of hearing them *every single day*, they became like nails on a chalkboard for me: Sheryl Crow's "A Change Would Do You Good," Fleetwood Mac's "Don't Stop," and Bruce Springsteen's "Born to Run." *Ugh*. Ruined forever.

Mr. Morgan wrapped the class up with Zuill Bailey playing a Bach cello piece. Perhaps he was building on the whole Bach-is-Friends's-signal-for-special-announcements thing. I was still humming the theme when Quint sidled up to my desk. "Ready for the mysterious assembly, Rhodes?" I realized that he was tapping his pen on the side of my desk in time with my humming and shut up. Quint is always tapping and drumming on every available surface—all that practice has made him the top percussionist in the school band.

"Yeah—is it going to be serious or something? They've never done a pop assembly since I've been here."

"Actually, the last one was to announce that you were coming here. Do you have any secret siblings who might be joining us?" he teased.

"Nope, no skeletons like that in my family's closet. Unfortunately for Madeline's grandpa." Quint rolled his eyes. He's so not into politics, at least not the us-versus-them kind. I grabbed my backpack and gestured toward the door. "Shall we?" We headed out, trailed by Hendrix.

We walked diagonally across the sunny commons, passing by a group of Lower School kids playing with a parachute on the grassy lawn. "There was one other surprise assembly last year," Quint said as we scuffed through curled-up leaves.

"Yeah? What for?"

"The class trip. That assembly happened about this time of year too." My heart sank. From the day I set foot on the Friends campus last winter, everyone was buzzing about the annual trip, which is to a different city each year. In May, the seventh grade went to Chicago. All spring I'd listened to my classmates debate signing up for the Cubs game over a day at the Shedd Aquarium, and then this fall I'd listened to them talk about how *awesome* the trip was on a freaking daily basis. I was the only student in my class who, for obvious reasons, couldn't go.

"Oh. You're probably right." We walked up the steps to Friendship Hall, which used to be a colonial church but now serves as the school's main auditorium. The first floor is filled with refurbished pews and up some stairs is a balcony that stretches along three sides of the large, one-room building. The back walls of the balcony level are broken up by the original stained-glass church windows, and on sunny days the seats up there are treated to a dazzling colored-light show. Quint and I hurried up the steps two at a time, seeing that the hall was already pretty full.

Seeing me plus Hendrix heading toward a front-row

balcony pew, the kids already sitting in it scooted their butts away, repelled like a drop of oil hitting water. Even though a lot of kids are still super fake-nice around me, not a lot of people want to sit next to a Secret Service agent at a boring assembly. It makes goofing off hard. Quint didn't seem to care, though. We settled into our pew, Hendrix taking a chair against the back wall behind us. A few minutes later the headmaster, Dr. Holmes, walked out to the pulpit-made-lectern. The crowd hushed.

"Good afternoon, students and Friends." He never resists that pun, and I could barely stifle a groan. Next to me, Quint rolled his eyes and pretended to gag. The way he was sitting, with his left leg crossed and resting on top of his right knee, I could see that he'd used a Sharpie to write "Here comes Treble" on the edge of his shoe. I found that unbearably adorkable.

"I'm very pleased to announce that the faculty council has decided on the destination for this year's class trip." I wished that I had the certainty of attending that everyone else had. *Maybe, if it's on the East Coast, I can go.* The room hushed as everyone waited for Dr. Holmes to announce the destination.

"This year's Friends Academy class trip will be to..." Dr. Holmes paused. For once he had the attention of every student during an assembly, and he milked it for all it was worth. "New York City!" The audience went crazy, cheers erupting and kids jumping up and down in the pews. "Careful, careful." Some of the teachers frantically ran around reminding people that they were in *a historic place* and needed to be *mindful of that*. Quint danced around in his seat, and I also found that adorkable.

His happiness was contagious, and I started to dance too. Sure, I'd been to New York a handful of times and seen the ballet and Broadway shows before. But I'd never been to 62nd and Madison and seen Bye's house. I wanted to see everyplace Alice had lived. I felt myself getting wrapped up in the excitement about the trip—until I remembered that I had roughly a snowball's chance in Hades of going. Last year, they decided it was too much of a security risk for me to travel with a school group. I didn't know how it would be any different this year, and New York is a big place. I slunk back down into my pew.

Quint turned to me, brown eyes shining. "Audrey, isn't that awesome? Maybe we'll get to see a performance of the Blue Man Group!" He started drumming on the seat of our pew with one hand and tapping the balcony ledge with the other.

I smiled halfheartedly. "Why haven't you seen it before? You go to New York with your parents a lot, right?" His dad is always at the UN, and his mom goes to all sorts of conferences and guest lectures.

"They're usually too busy for stuff like that. And if we go to a concert or a show, they only like serious stuff."

"I can relate—" I was interrupted by Dr. Holmes speaking again.

"I'm glad to see such enthusiasm for our selection. The itinerary is still being finalized, but we do intend to offer chances to see live theater, tour the museums, and perhaps even pay a visit to Lady Liberty." He explained that we'd all receive an informational packet at home to share with our parents. A limited number of scholarships would be available for students in need of financial assistance to attend. Friends Academy did have a few students in each grade enrolled through merit scholarships, and to the school's credit, every effort is made to allow them to have the same experience at school as their privileged counterparts.

When the assembly wrapped up, everyone spilled out of the hall into the commons, splintering into cliques to collectively freak out about how cool the trip was this year. A few of Quint's friends wandered over, and pretty soon all of the eighth-graders crowded together, talking about the trip. Madeline sauntered over to where Quint and I stood. She and Quint had band in common—Madeline played clarinet. I cursed myself for never picking up an instrument. Ignoring me, Madeline asked him, "Do you think we'll get to go to Carnegie Hall? Or hear the Philharmonic?"

"That would be so cool. I wanna go check the concert schedule…" Quint trailed off. Madeline and some other band members closed in a circle around him, and I stood off to the outside. I slouched there, imagining what traipsing around New York with Quint would be like. I could picture us strolling through Central Park together, or maybe taking one of those rowboats for a spin. I imagined us sharing an armrest as we watched ballet at Lincoln Center. I saw us taking pictures of each other with the Statue of Liberty or Times Square in the background. Then I looked back at him talking to Madeline and reimagined all those scenes with Madeline replacing me. And I wanted to puke. *I have to go on the New York trip. Seriously.* I started to brainstorm reasons why I should go, making a list of talking points for my mom. What did Alice call her little trip to christen the yacht in New York? A *boon* to the presidency? I could tell my mom that me going to New York would help her too. I just wasn't sure how, other than promising to be well-behaved.

When I got home from school, I made a beeline for my mom's office. "Denise, I need to talk to my mom," I begged. Denise was the gatekeeper to my mom's office—even when it was me trying to get in.

"Your mother is preparing for an important call," Denise answered, barely looking up from a handful of memos.

"This is an emergency!" I am the Girl Who Cried Emergency, but only out of necessity. That's the only way to get through Denise.

Denise sighed. "Okay, you can go in for a minute." She pressed the intercom on the secretary's desk. "Madam President, your daughter would like a word."

I burst in and ran up to my mother's desk. "Mom, I *have* to go to New York."

"Huh? Right now?" My mom pulled off her reading glasses, confused.

"No, this spring. The school trip. They announced it today. We'll get an info packet soon." I bit my lip. "Please just say I can go. I think it would be a good publicity thing for you. If I…" I thought for a second. "Went to the Statue of Liberty! Ellis Island! Think of the photo ops. It could make up for Bikinigate."

"Honey," my mother started. "Obviously I'll look at the information. But the concerns that kept you from going to Chicago last spring haven't gone away." She frowned sympathetically. "I have to be honest—it's very unlikely. Your dad and I simply aren't comfortable with you going on a school trip, even with your security. But we could plan a trip for you and I to take together. I have some fund-raisers to do—"

"You don't understand!" My voice cracked. "It's not the place. It's getting to go with everyone from school." Visions of Quint and Madeline and everyone else having a ball, without me, danced through my head. I wanted a chance to be a normal kid on a school trip so badly. Those kinds of trips are when everybody bonds and inside jokes are born. I *needed* to be a part of that. "I have to go. Please," I pleaded.

"I do understand. But we're all making sacrifices here, honey." *But you chose to make them,* I wanted to scream. *I was never free to do that!*

"*Ugh!*" I stomped my foot. "You don't get anything."

"Audrey, that's not fair."

"Neither is ninety-five percent of my current life." I turned on my heel and headed out of the room.

"Audrey," my mom called after me, but I ignored her. I pushed past Denise, who was waiting on the other side of the door.

I ran upstairs and slammed my door. First thing, I turned on some music to relax. Classical, while I stretched—but no special-announcement Bach because that would only upset me more. Then I turned on the playlist my dance teacher gave me before I moved, and I danced around my room for as long as it took to feel calm. It didn't last, though, because when I flopped on the floor, sweaty and exhausted, I couldn't stop thinking about a trip I wouldn't take and the friendships I wouldn't make. *Nobody gets what I have to go through as a First Kid.* Nobody. *Well, except Alice.* I reached over and slid the diary out of my desk drawer. It felt weird to be hiding someone else's diary. But if I showed it to my parents, they'd probably find a way to ruin it too. No way would I let that happen. I thumbed through the musty pages to the one I'd left off at, when Alice was flush from her yacht christening in New York Harbor. Lucky girl.

February 28, 1902
Diary—

First, if any of my maids are reading this entry, I swear on my mother's grave that I will seek revenge on you! I caught a maid peeking in this very journal the other day. I was flabbergasted. I may scoff at my stepmother's obsession with privacy, but when it comes to my diary, I believe in it too! I refuse to censor myself, but perhaps I will have to devise ways to protect my most private confessions from prying eyes. Maybe you've noticed already (you'd have to be blind not to have), but I'm trying to use Bye's peculiar style of handwriting here. She slants her letters to an almost unreadable degree. It's an awful lot of effort, though, and so far I'm imitating her style with a singular lack of success.

I am so very glum today. Despite my fantastic job at foreign relations with our German friends, Father is not allowing me to attend Edward VII's coronation.

When we received the invitation, I jumped and ran the long hallway upstairs and did somersaults, terrifying some of our menagerie (as evidenced by Eli's squawks) as I cartwheeled into the Conservatory. That giddiness was short-lived. As soon as the papers caught wind, the White House was besieged with mail, from constituents who found it "inappropriate" for me to be lumped in with royalty. My father was sorry for me, but he explained that although some (mainly those already in favor of his administration) would not care if I went, many (mainly the fools in opposition to him) would be very, very upset. I don't like feeling like a pawn in the chess game that is his administration. This is precisely why politics frustrate me—they have a nasty way of getting in the way of living. Sure, I want to be a boon to my father's presidency, but I bristle at his presidency hindering my life. He tried to tell me that I was a great help with the Kaiser's yacht, and I can help again by not going to the coronation. But! Going to the coronation is the stuff of my wildest dreams. If I had the ability and the power to choose in this situation, I would choose for myself and go.

To Thine Own Self be True,
Alice

March 2, 1902
Diary—

My ashen spirits are rising like a phoenix. I may not be able to go to England for Edward VII's coronation, but I am about to embark on a "consolation trip" to Cuba! I'll spend a month on the island doing all sorts of diplomatic chores for Father. I leave in only a few days. I have trunks upon trunks to pack, and Stepmother is constantly fussing over me, making sure that I bring everything I ought to and also giving me little subtle suggestions of how I should comport myself when I am there. I will not give her the satisfaction of making this pledge aloud, but I do intend to make my family proud, so long as Roosevelt pride and great experiences are not in opposition to each other.

Once my ship has set sail, I will have more time to write. But for now, I must pack and prepare. And teach Ethel how to feed Emily Spinach bits of fish and earthworms from the South Lawn.

Be True, and Bon voyage!
Alice

March 12, 1902
Diary—

*I haven't had a dull moment since we chugged out
of New York Harbor. Do you know how absolutely
invigorating it is to stand upon the deck of a great ship
and watch your country fade behind you? To let your
arms trail in the briny breeze and feel the salty spray
cover your face? To know that you are setting out to
see the world and soak up all the liveliness and love
it has to offer? It feels like freedom incarnate. Even
after the harbor's crowds faded and the rest of the
delegation settled into their compartments belowdecks,
I stood out near the rails and watched the sea sputter
and churn. This is what I have needed for so long—a
chance to get away from all the rules of my household
and the tiny sphere of Washington and eat up more of
the world. A great, big, heaping helping of life.*

*Forgive me for babbling; I am simply mad for
travel. As I write, I am already on the island of Cuba.
It is a lush, steamy, and wild place. Not that my
escapades here are wild—they are mostly diplomatic
and I am behaving myself. My chaperone is one of
the governesses from the White House, Annabelle
Alsop. While she's not the most fuss-box chaperone*

I've encountered, she keeps too close of an eye on me for my taste.

My days are full of little State-business adventures, like visiting a school for poor little orphans. My heart ached for all those little motherless rascals, perhaps because I halfway share their losses. But I've also attended charity receptions, teas, and parties. The army gave a cavalry review in my honor, which made me blush terribly, but I managed to stammer out some words to the handsome soldiers.

Speaking of handsome—I hesitate to tell you, for fear of more snooping from my maids back in Washington—but I must or my heart will burst. I have a beau. Edward Carpenter, one of the aides to Major General Wood. I fell in love at first sight with his uniform, and it did not take long at all for his sense of humor to win me over too. His blond hair is cut in the typical military fashion, he has an almost perfectly straight nose, he has wonderfully broad shoulders, he is taller than I am, and he has beautiful sparkling blue eyes. One side of his mouth, the right, curls up noticeably more than the left when he smiles. It makes his smile even more dashing. He is so proper that he calls me only "Miss Roosevelt." I break with tradition and call him "Carpenter." When he says "Roosevelt," it

Rebecca Behrens

sounds like an incantation—or at least it has put me in a trance. He slipped me a note at dinner the other night. Trembling, I unfolded it. What sweet nothings might it contain? It read: "As I have nothing to do, I'll write. As I have nothing to say, I'll close." I burst out laughing amidst the stares of our dinner companions. I love Carpenter's wit; Diary, I do think I may love him. I will keep you closely posted on my interactions with my dear Edward.

Other than swooning over my darling, I have taken a great interest in the game of jai alai. It is the sport here in Cuba—players hurl balls between each other, catching them in these odd little baskets called cestas. The game itself is not as interesting as baseball, but gambling on games makes jai alai bully fun. I do adore placing bets on the matches, and I am doing quite well for myself.

To Thine Own Self Be True,
Alice

March 20, 1902
Diary—

I have a moment free to write because my chaperone Annabelle has taken ill after we ate too much spicy

Cuban food. Poor woman, she hasn't got a cast-iron stomach like I do. I can't help it—I insist that we indulge in the local delicacies at every meal. My favorite thing to eat is "Congri," a mixture of red beans and rice. Father ate it when he was here with the Rough Riders and told me to try it. You eat it with ripe and sweet plantains. The best sauce I've tried is Mojo, which combines lime, garlic, onions, and oregano in oil. It's delicious. Oh, and I've stuffed myself with more tamales than I can possibly count. As much as I love consommé and soufflé, this Cuban chuck might be better.

If I were a good daughter of the president, I would be filling you with tales of schools visited, sugar plantations toured, and yellow-fever mosquitoes swatted. Alas, I am a somewhat naughty daughter of the president and all I can think to tell you about is my dear Carpenter. What a hold he has over me. Heaven is watching him break into his lopsided smile for me, as a shock of his blond hair falls into his blue eyes and he brushes it away. I spend every possible moment with him, although Annabelle is constantly present. (I know the rules that must be obeyed for a girl of my class and political situation—one mustn't even emerge from a dance hall with her hair disheveled or *a button innocently askew lest the rumors fly. Never mind that with the elaborate hairstyles du jour, it's frightfully tricky to keep up appearances even in the most mundane and innocent circumstances.)*

I worry, though, that Carpenter will grow tired of me or that he will discover how contrary and difficult a person I am (just ask my stepmother for confirmation). When will he abandon me, as everyone in my life eventually does? He accuses me of having a temper, which is true, and then I grovel, grovel, beg, and plead, so terrified am I that I have driven him away. When I'm with him, and not distracted by his handsome shoulders or good-fitting uniform, all I can think about is this desperate need to make sure he finds me beautiful and charming. Doubt gnaws at me—what if he thinks that a courtship with me will lead to great things for his career? What if that's the real reason he's interested in a plain girl with a gargantuan forehead and formerly crippled legs? And then there is the constant threat posed by one of my traveling companions, the lovely (wretched!) Janet Lee, whom I can tell Edward fancies by how he looks at her porcelain face. Being the president's daughter can't get a girl Janet Lee's beauty. I can never truly tell whether anyone fancies me because of who I am or because my father is Father. Deep down, I fear I am not quite pretty enough, or witty enough, on my own to garner much attention. And so I cling to the crumbs that fall my way.

We have little time left in Cuba. I will tour another sugar plantation, attend another ball, and then back to the United States we shall go. I hope Carpenter's favor travels with me.

To Thine Own Self Be True,
Alice

March 24, 1902
Diary—

I have left the magical island of Cuba in my wake, quite literally. As my ship prepared to leave the port, a crowd of friends that I had made on this bully fun trip came to see me off. After all the others had said their merry good-byes, Edward hung back. We had a few precious moments alone on the boat (I had to wait until Annabelle and the rest of our entourage were busy attending to the luggage). Carpenter seemed as melancholy as I felt, sighing and struggling to keep the lopsided corners of his delightfully masculine mouth from turning ever downward. We stood on a secluded part of the deck, the breeze whipping our hair and the sun shining in our faces. "Here, Miss Roosevelt," he said, as he pressed a few photographs of himself (in his uniform!) into my palm. "I beg of you to write me, and often." I said I would, and with "yearning." I spoke in jest, but I still blushed and so did he. Then it was time for us to set sail, and he disembarked. I retreated to my compartment, where I sobbed pitifully. Janet and Annabelle bid me to come out on deck, but I staunchly refused. I even missed watching us leave the harbor, which I do somewhat regret now. It would've been nice to see Cuba fade away on the horizon.

Now, of course, we are near to America. Having been abroad and free, I imagine it won't be easy to be back under my parents' roof and abiding by their rules constantly. This trip, plus my excellent performance with the christening of the yacht, should show them that they should let me taste a little more of the world even whilst I'm at home.

To Thine Own Self Be True,
Alice

Chapter 8

I'd been ready to give up on the New York trip—my mom doesn't flip-flop on saying *no* to something. Two things made me decide to keep trying: Alice's diary and a heart-to-heart with Debra. At first, the entry in which Alice bemoaned not being able to go to the coronation had me convinced that so long as I was a First Kid, I wouldn't be doing much solo travel. But just as Alice's spirits "rose like a phoenix" (and I knew what that meant, thanks to Harry Potter), so did mine as I read on. Alice managed to get her parents to send her *all the way to Cuba*! I was *not* surprised that a First Daughter found love only while she was away from the White House. Quint would be on the New York trip; maybe travel would work the same magic for me. Chugging out of New York Harbor invigorated Alice, and I wanted to chug into it. Or drive, I guess, because you can't take a boat there from DC.

Then one night I found myself sitting at the kitchen

counter, working on my homework while watching Debra make pancakes for my dinner. Except I couldn't focus on my French verbs because I was obsessing about two things: the trip and Quint.

"Sweetness, you don't seem yourself today." Debra didn't look up at me but kept stirring a bowl of batter furiously. She poured a cupful onto a sizzling-hot griddle.

At that point, I hadn't told anyone about my crush on Quint. Which had only been growing. I felt like it was a balloon blowing up inside me, and if it got much bigger, it would cause me to burst. But I shrugged off her question.

"Nuh-uh. Something's on your mind. I need to hear all about it." Debra looked up at me and smiled, her twinkling blue eyes full of understanding.

Debra actually listens. "Okay, I've got a huge secret, and it's eating me up inside," I exclaimed, throwing my arms across the countertop and laying my head down on them in mock exhaustion. "You promise you won't tell anyone?"

Debra wiped the edge of the bowl on a towel and set both down. "It's like I went to the *other* CIA. I know how to keep mum."

I couldn't help but grin. "Where to start? Two things are driving me crazy. One, I *need* to get permission to go on the class trip. And two, I have..." I paused, then squeezed my eyes shut and blurted it out in one breath.

"A-massive-crush-on-this-guy-Quint." It felt *so* great to tell someone that.

I opened my eyes and looked up at Debra. Her hands were clasped in glee. "Pictures! I need to see some pictures." So I ran upstairs to grab First Friend Laptop, then pulled up photos of Quint on Facebook to show her.

"Such a cutie! This is so exciting. I bet he likes you too. What boy wouldn't?" She winked and flipped a few pancakes onto a plate.

"So how do I get permission to go on the trip? That's my big chance to hang out with Quint. My parents are treating me like I'm a thirteen-year-old baby."

Debra put the plate in front of me and sat down on her stool across the counter. She furrowed her eyebrows. "Be honest and explain to your parents how important this trip is to you. Promise them that you'll play by all the rules. I know you'd do that anyway, but they need reassurance. They're your parents, and they can't help but worry about their little girl. Even if you're not so little anymore."

Debra understood that I wasn't a kid anymore, at least. I jumped up and ran around the counter to give her a huge hug.

I tried selling my dad on the trip, without success. "It's too difficult in terms of the security logistics," he explained. "You'd need more than two agents to go with you, and there would be so many press and paparazzi restrictions. We're already under fire from Mom's opponents for travel expenses. It wouldn't look good." He suggested we go to Camp David the week of the class trip, if I didn't want to stay behind in DC. *A consolation trip. Cuba was supposed to be one for Alice. Should I take this offer?* Camp David's nice, but a trip to the Big Apple with my classmates it's not. *Nope!*

The following week, my dad needed to attend the opening of a new DC charter school and asked me if I'd mind missing classes for a day to come along. My first thought was that opening a school might be sort of like christening a yacht—both were ceremonies to celebrate something new. Although nobody would get to crack a bottle of champagne on a school wall, it could still be fun. And this was a rare opportunity. My dad spends little time in the Kitchen Garden staging First Gent photo ops, or writing children's books, or even advising my mom. Denise and Susan Pierpont started urging him to take a more active role and amp up his platform: education. "It looks like you're shirking your First Gentleman responsibilities. We definitely don't want to start *another* gender debate," Denise explained. Added Susan, "I can barely keep up with the requests. We need to start saying yes to at least some." Dad agreed, begrudgingly, to a few appearances before the holidays, when our whole family would be celebrating on the national stage.

I reported to his official office (separate from his 1600 lab space) in the East Wing around 11:30. Although its name changed from "First Lady's Office" once we moved in, people still screw up all the time and call it that. But my dad has a pretty good sense of humor about being called a *First Lady*. "Hi," I said, stepping into the room. Staffers milled around, like always. They all nodded or waved hello to acknowledge me, then went back to pecking on their laptops.

My dad walked in a few seconds later. "What do I need to know for this event? Who's running the school? Is it named after a figure I should be familiar with?" The aides circled around him with memos and clipboards. I plopped down in a leather chair and pulled out *Great Expectations*, which my English class was reading. I remembered Alice writing something about the White House looking like Miss Havisham's, so she must've read it too. I liked thinking of us sharing a book.

"Ready to go, Audrey?" I looked up and saw Nick Appiah, the Director of Policy and Projects for the First Gentleman, standing near the door. My dad, Susan, and a few other aides were already on their way out to the motorcade. "Yeah, sorry." I threw my book in my bag and headed out, feeling more like an afterthought than usual. When my dad had invited me, somehow I'd thought this visit would be a little more like quality father-daughter time and less like another photo op for which I was the stock family prop.

❧

The school was on Fifth and Florida NE, in a part of DC that I had never been in—although I haven't been in much of DC, actually. I gazed out the SUV's window as we rolled through the city, drinking in all the different neighborhoods. We sped down a street with no fewer than four Ethiopian restaurants. Whenever I visit them, Uncle Harrison and Max take me to their favorite place for injera and lentils and honey wine. Well, they have the honey wine and I have water, but Harrison let me take a sip once. The car turned off the restaurant row and onto a street with tons of shoppers picking through stuff lying out on folding tables. I felt jealous of the pedestrians walking around, despite the fact that there was a typical early December chill in the air. I only walk on the Friends campus or the White House grounds.

The redbrick school was shiny, modern, and had tons of windows and skylights. There was a sparse vegetable garden to its left and a playground to its right. "Is this an elementary school?" I asked, looking at the brightly colored play equipment.

"For now. It'll be K–12 eventually, and already has

high-tech science labs and athletic facilities," Nick answered. "Your dad has such an inspiring science career. We want to highlight that this school will produce future scholars of his level." Nick always works what sound like campaign talking points into ordinary conversation. Total politician-in-training.

We sat and waited to exit the vehicle. Some members of the press congregated outside, along with school officials and some tiny kids in school uniforms. Finally, we got the go-ahead, and my dad reluctantly put away his tablet. "Let's go open a school, Audrey."

As soon as we stepped out, the crowd became a mess of handshakes and introductions and people fawning over the First Gent. I stood off to the side, awkwardly, having total déjà vu of standing outside the circle of Quint and his friends after the assembly. For the longest time, everyone ignored me. I looked down at my pale arms, examining all my freckles. Sometimes the world seemed so far away from me that I needed to do that—stare at my arms, or something—to reassure myself that I was still a part of it. That I hadn't somehow morphed into a ghost overnight and the reason I float through life by myself isn't that I'm dead or something. I pinched my forearm, and the skin flashed white, then red. *Just checking.* Finally Nick must've remembered me, and he called me over to meet the school principal.

The small crowd quieted down so my father could give a few opening remarks—*"Schools like this are what make our country great, because we invest in our children and the lives of their minds."* I watched my dad, noticing how different it was to see him schmooze a group. His eye contact needed work. My mom's eyes seem to recognize people even if she's never laid eyes on them before; she's a natural crowd-pleaser. Like my dad, I have to work at winning people over or getting their attention.

After Dad raced through his prepared remarks, we headed off on the grand tour. Susan and the principal were in the middle of a passive-aggressive battle of who would lead the group, one constantly stepping in front of the other. My father trailed them with Nick, who was whispering in his ear pertinent information about the school's features so Dad could compliment them. A couple of reporters and a photographer hovered near them. I lagged behind. The staffer assigned to monitor me obsessively scrolled to read something on her phone whenever we weren't moving from room to room. I crossed and recrossed my arms over my chest and huffed. I couldn't imagine Alice being in a situation like this, being ignored by a room full of people.

We headed into the bright and airy new library. A bunch of adorable little kids in spotless uniforms gathered around a young librarian. She was holding a copy of some picture book and smiling nervously. The kids' eyes widened as our group filed into the room. They were so young that one girl was even sucking on her thumb as she sat cross-legged on the story-time rug.

"I think it's time for a reading." Susan grinned at me. "Go ahead, Audrey." She motioned me toward the seated kids. *I'm doing the reading?* I was startled for a minute, but another look at the cute kids reassured me. It would be like reading to the kids I used to babysit in St. Paul. They always loved the voices I did for different characters. *I bet these kids will love them too. Then all the journalists can go home and write a glowing piece about the charming and poised First Daughter and how much the children of the charter school loved her story-reading skills.* Alice visited schools in Cuba as part of her tour, and I bet that was one of the things that convinced her parents that her trips were useful.

Grinning, I walked right up to the librarian and reached for the book. She kept it pressed firmly against her trembling knees. *I guess she's so nervous that she's freezing up? Poor lady.* It must be pretty intimidating to have people from the White House in your workplace. To help her out, I grabbed hold of the book and tried to gently pry it away. She shot me a confused look and held tight to the opposite side. Both still smiling, we started the world's weirdest book tug-of-war. Everyone stood silently, watching us. Out of the corner of my eye, I saw Nick whisper to Susan and then quietly start walking over toward me.

"*Audrey!*" he hissed. "Sit down and let her read!" He motioned to the floor, as though I'm too dumb to understand what "sit down" means.

I clenched my teeth and hissed back, "But then what am I here for?"

Nick softly pleaded, "To listen to the story!"

Shocked, I dropped my half of the book, and the poor librarian almost toppled over. My face burned with irritation, and I sunk to the floor without making eye contact with anyone in the crowd. The librarian started reading in a shaky voice. "Once upon a time, there was a little girl. Her mother told her she could be whatever she dreamed of when she grew up. A dancer. An artist. A doctor. Even the president. That sounded best to the little girl. But when she told all her friends that she wanted to run the country some day, they just laughed and laughed..." Of course they were reading a picture book about my mom. *To me.*

I glanced up at my dad, to see if he found this whole thing as absurd as I did. He smiled back at me, and the worst part was he looked *reassuring.* Like he thought I might feel embarrassed by mistakenly thinking that I should be the one reading the book. *The people running this thing should be embarrassed, not me!* In what universe would treating a thirteen-year-old like a kindergartner *not* be obnoxious? I sat on the rug and fumed. Every time I heard a camera shutter snap, my mouth set deeper in a frown.

The instant story time was over, I hopped on my feet and made a beeline for the door, even as the rest of the entourage stood around admiring the skylights and lofted reading nooks. "Where are you going?" the phone-obsessed aide asked me.

"None of your business," I snapped, brushing past her. The reporter looked up from her notepad and watched as I stomped out of the room, still scowling.

"Audrey!" The aide trailed after me into the hallway. "Hold up!" I kept walking down the hallway, breaking into a run as soon as I turned a corner. I pushed open the first door I saw. It led to the pool.

It was a fantastic space—more like an atrium and less like the basement YMCA pool deck where I had taken swimming lessons in Minnesota. The tiles glittered and plantings lined the walls like it was a greenhouse. The humid air smelled fresh and slightly like eucalyptus, with undertones of chlorine. I paused for a moment and inhaled deeply, closing my eyes. The only sound in the room was the soft echo of the waves hitting the pool's ledge and the slurp of the drain. The sound of the water reminded me of the ocean and Alice's comment about standing on the deck and feeling so invigorated. *Why was Alice's life so different from mine?* She lived at a time when women couldn't *vote* but in some ways she seemed so much freer than me. I couldn't wear a two-piece swimsuit. I couldn't pick out my own clothes. I couldn't go on awesome trips. Alice got to grow up in the White House, but I felt like I was growing back toward the kids on the story-time rug. No—*I* wasn't growing backward, but the people in charge of my life were trying to freeze me in childhood like a fly in amber. I had to find some way to stop them.

The staffer who'd been chasing after me barged in. "Audrey! What's going on?"

I turned toward her and away from the pool. "I needed some space."

She nodded, not unsympathetically. "Are you okay to go back?"

"Sure."

"The art room is next." *They better not try to make me finger paint.*

April 13, 1902
Diary—

Life has been a bore since I returned from Cuba. Yet I must have learned something while I was abroad because I am much more willing now to "fulfill my role" as the First Daughter. My father wrote me, saying, "You were of real service down there because you made those people feel that you liked them and took an interest in them, and your presence was accepted as a great compliment." I think my stepmother worries a smidgen less about my wild behavior. Thus far, it is making daily life in the White House a little more harmonious.

Adding some heft to the idea of Alice as an asset and not a liability, the Ladies' Home Journal published a most flattering profile of me once I returned. It took up a full page and even featured an illustration of me, which I imagine might be clipped and tacked to the walls of many young girls' bedrooms. "The typical American girl of good health and sane ideas" was one gushing compliment. Little do they know about my actual degree of sanity. At another point, they called me "gracefully slender." I chuckle reading that, ruminating both on the gobs of Cuban food I stuffed myself with last month and also those hideous leg braces. After all these years, I swear I still feel them clasping my legs.

*I read the article and pored over the illustration—
which was beautiful, but really didn't resemble me. It
bore my features, for better or worse, but it was some
other, more beautiful, more assured Alice. After I
put it down, I took my Spanish white lace mantilla
out of my trunk. At first just to run my fingers over
the finery, but then something compelled me to put it
on. I locked the door, because I would die of embarrassment if Ethel or one of the boys would barge in
and see me playing dress-up like a little girl. But no
one saw me. I struggled into my best dress (omitting
my usual formal undergarments did not make it any
easier) and sat in front of my vanity. I tamed my hair
in some approximation of the Cuban styles I'd seen,
and framed it with the lace dripping from my head
onto my shoulders. Then I paraded in front of my
mirror, watching the fabric move and marveling at
how I looked wearing it.*

*I know I must sound beyond vain. But I simply am
trying to see what the world finds captivating about
me—and even wearing roses and Spanish lace, I can't
see what the fuss is about. My vanity is all bluster. If
I were not the president's daughter, I simply would be
another homely girl, even when dressed up in finery.*

I wonder too, what my Edward sees in me. Can

I ever trust his affection? In Cuba I would only just convince myself that he only had eyes for me when I would catch him admiring Janet or some trollop. Then doubt would creep into the corners of my mind. I put on the dress and wanted to see what Edward saw in me; I wanted to see if it could be true that it really was Alice alone that captivated him.

To Thine Own Self Be True,
Alice

April 25, 1902
Diary—

Most young ladies ride around town in a carriage. I have long taken to careening down Connecticut Avenue on my bicycle (oftentimes with my legs up on the handlebars to shock the passerby). But as a modern and mature young woman, a bicycle is simply no longer enough. I used some of my generous Lee allowance to purchase a runabout, a bright-red little open automobile. I drive it alone on short jaunts around the city. Ladies aren't supposed to drive alone, but I won't have anyone handle my "Red Devil" but me. Try to stop me—you'll have to run fast. I am ace at driving it. *I have already been stopped once for excessive speed (it scares the horses). I tried to talk my way out of the fine, but apparently even the president's daughter must obey the traffic laws.*

I like to take my new friend Maggie Cassini out driving with me. I met Maggie, the niece of the Russian ambassador, at a State Dinner. I came into the room with Emily Spinach wrapped around my neck, and Maggie hurried right over to try her on for herself. I think it goes without saying that we hit it off immediately.

Maggie, despite being young, functions as the ambassadress for her uncle. You can imagine the protests surrounding that—an unmarried woman as ambassadress—but Maggie overcame them. She hosts the liveliest Sunday evening dinner parties at their residence on Rhode Island Avenue. She's my only real competition for attention in our social circle, but I consider her a worthy opponent.

I taught Maggie how to drive, and in exchange she has promised to teach me some scandalous new dances (like the hootchy-kootchy, but European, and even racier). Maggie is a kindred spirit indeed, a fellow seeker of thrills and experiences. She's a breath of fresh air—unlike some of my Puritanical girlfriends (cough,

cough—Janet Lee). They care about appearances and manners and comportment; Maggie cares about having fun. Nothing shocks her. The only trouble is that she is very beautiful and wealthy, a Russian countess, so I may have to dip more into my Lee funds to keep up with her. She is certainly someone I want to keep up with, though. Every girl needs a dear friend, as much for sharing secrets as for sharing in mischief.

To Thine Own Self Be True,
Alice

One thing I love about 1600: the holidays. I love the greenery—they seriously turn this place into an indoor forest with all the fir and pine and holly. I love doing all of the tree-lighting and school-group-caroling traditions with my parents, even if they are in front of huge audiences and popping flashbulbs. I spend hours down in the chocolate shop, watching (and sometimes assisting) with the construction of the official White House gingerbread house. At my request, the houses had a Victorian theme this year. Debra and I spent hours hand-making candies for them after school. I decorated one of the little marzipan people to be Alice Roosevelt. People kept asking why I painted a green snake over her shoulders, but I didn't explain.

The best part, though, was that my family escaped back to Minnesota for a full week. Harrison came up from Wisconsin to get our house ready for us, turning on the heat and shoveling and such. Max baked all of my favorite Christmas cookies in advance. When our motorcade pulled up to the long driveway on a frigid Minnesota December evening, tons of twinkling Christmas lights and wreaths welcomed us. Seeing my old house looking so lived-in brought tears to my eyes, which I pretended were from the cold. "We're home!" I yelled and jumped out of the car, running up the walk. Harrison stood shivering on the front stoop with a cup of cocoa for me, and before we opened the door to rush inside, Kim pulled it open.

"AHHHHHHHHHHHHHHHHHHHHH!" I screamed.

"AHHHHHHHHHHHHHHHHHHHHHH!" Kim screamed back. We danced around the front hall hugging, me tracking snow and leaving little puddles everywhere. I had *my* Maggie Cassini back.

The visit flew by, and before I knew it, it was our last night at home. I had ignored the reality of going back to DC until then, when I fell into a huge funk. I liked being in my old house. I liked the freedom to make a mess in my kitchen and blast my music without worrying that someone would be bothered. I loved being able to walk over to Kim's house at a moment's notice, even if an agent followed me there. The thought of going back to rigid, lonely 1600 life bummed me out. Even Kim coming over couldn't pull me out of my bad mood. We were standing in the kitchen, taking a break from one of our bake-fests, and Kim was licking cookie dough off a mixer. "What's wrong?" she asked.

"You're going to get salmonella," I said.

"Don't try to distract me, and salmonella is worth this deliciousness." Kim stuck out her dough-covered tongue, and I cringed.

I sighed. "I'm not ready to go back and face the social Sahara again."

"How are you not the most popular girl at school? You're the freaking president's kid."

"That's the thing," I said, shaking my head. "I can never tell when people actually like me or if they want to suck up to the Fido. It's superhard to make *real* friends when everybody is faux-nice to you. Except Madeline." If nothing else, she was consistently bratty.

"So take advantage of their fake niceness. You'll never have to worry about not having someone to go to a dance with."

I laughed, thinking of the one dance I went to, right after I started at Friends. "Imagine going to a dance and being shadowed by a Secret Service agent the whole time. Everyone ran away from me like I was Pepé Le Pew!"

"Are you sure you're not like, projecting or something? Maybe that dance you went to last spring was awkward because you were new."

"Kim, I spent ninety percent of it slouching by the snack

table with my agents. I danced once with Chris Whitman, and that's probably another reason why Madeline hates me so much."

"So what about your friend Quint? You talk to him and stuff."

Hearing his name made me blush. "Yeah, we're cool. I was really hoping we could hang out together on the New York trip..." I trailed off, thinking about Quint picking out excursions with me in mind. I got so distracted that I slammed a mixing bowl on the counter a little too heavily and made Kim jump. "Sorry. Uh, anyway...tell me more about you and Taylor."

Kim happily launched into talking about her recently acquired boyfriend and the gifts they'd gotten each other for Christmas. I gazed out the window as Kim chattered away, watching the snow falling on my backyard. I pictured myself running around in it, making snow sculptures like I used to as a kid, but instead of picturing Kim making them with me I thought of Quint. I could imagine snowflakes getting caught on his thick eyelashes and covering his curly mop of hair, in stark contrast to its rich brown color. My first kiss, with Paul, actually had been in the middle of a snowball fight. *What would it be like to kiss Quint...*

"Audrey?" My father was standing in the kitchen doorway, and I hadn't even noticed.

"Want a cookie?" I asked, and Kim offered him the plate.

"Thanks," he said, popping one in his mouth. "*Mmm*, delicious. Did Max give you the recipe for these?" I nodded. "I'm heading to bed, and I'm sure your mom will be soon too. You girls can stay up as late as you like, but keep in mind you're going to be up at the crack—we leave at six tomorrow morning."

"Okay. We'll be quiet," I said.

"Good girls. It was wonderful to see you, Kimmy," my dad said, giving Kim a quick hug before heading upstairs.

"I guess I should let you get some sleep, huh?" Kim smiled sadly.

"No!" I exclaimed, louder than I'd meant to. "I mean, I don't want you to go." I felt my eyes welling with tears. *Ugh, don't start crying. Toughen up.*

"Aw, Audrey." Kim stopped shrugging into her coat and leaned over to give me a hug. "You just have to come back more to visit."

"Or you need to visit DC!"

"I'll try. I'm training for track in the spring, so I'll be superbusy then, though." Kim shoved a knit hat on her head and slipped her feet into thick boots. "Walk me out?" I nodded and threw on some boots too, and we headed out to the stoop. We said good night to the agent posted at the front door, who looked on as I walked Kim down to the sidewalk and hugged her tightly. "I'll miss you, K!" Tears rolled down my face as I watched Kim trudge off through the swirling snow.

I ran back up to my real bedroom and zipped open the hidden compartment in my suitcase, pulling out Alice's diary. So what if I'd have to be up in a few short hours? I needed her voice to keep me company. I was in the storm of a dark mood, as she'd describe it.

May 12, 1902
Diary—

I'm afraid I've had a foolish temper fit with my step-mother. I acted more like little Ethel would, stomping my feet and storming out of the room. Then Edith snidely remarked that I should thank her for the use of my legs—referring to how she helped me stretch them every night when I wore the braces. I would moan and cry and resist, but Edith wouldn't take no for an answer, telling me that if I endured the discomfort, I'd have normal, ladylike legs one day. Stepmother loves to take credit for the fact that I am graceful now, and I hate to admit that she deserves it.

Our scuffle today wasn't my fault, though! Edith got absolutely livid about a newspaper story concerning me. It said two different men were in love with me and that I was "toying" with both. The story was full of downright lies, of course—the only man I have eyes for right now is my Edward, whom the papers have never written about. What the reporters write about me is primarily fiction, and I can't be bothered with it. (Frankly, the falsehoods are a lot more entertaining to read than the truth of my life.) My fuss-box father and stepmother, on the other hand—they are horrified by what the papers say.

Of course, I barely see my father these days. I know whom I can blame at present—the petulant coal workers finally went on strike today, and now both the unions and the mine owners are clamoring for my father to intervene. The bottom line for me is that he will be unable to intervene in his own family's lives for the time being, as he lives and breathes this crisis. My father abandoned me once before when there was too much in his life for him to pay attention to me, so I suppose it's not unreasonable for me to fear that he might again.

Bye tells me that I push boundaries because otherwise I fear nobody will notice me. (She's an astute judge of character.) I always have to fight for my father's attention, if not his love. This adoration and *admiration from the public and the press—I don't need to battle for it. I simply have to step out the front door and wave. Toss them a smile, and they love me for life. Tell me, if you were me, which would you choose? A life spent quietly inside the White House or one played out on the world's stage? See, I am not so rotten and scandalous. I always say, "Fill what's empty, empty what's full, and scratch where it itches." I'm full up of disapproval at home and empty of sufficient love. Morever, I itch for experience.*

To Thine Own Self Be True,
Alice

May 16, 1902
Diary—

A quick dispatch for you on the subject of: cigarettes. My marvelous friend Maggie recently has taught me the art of smoking. It took some instruction—the first breaths I took of tobacco smoke were shaky, leading to coughing fits as soon as I expelled the cloud from my otherwise hardy lungs. Honestly, the experience of cajoling smoke into one's mouth and throat conjures little pleasure in me. It's harsh, sticky, and acrid; it coats your mouth and throat in a very disagreeable way. Maggie is such an expert that she can blow the smoke out of her mouth in distinct lines and shapes. I'm not sure I'll become the aficionado she is, but I'm looking forward to the next time the men at a dinner party gather in a den or library for smoking and political discourse—I suppose I will join in, blow a smoke ring or two, and shock the lot of them. No woman has ever smoked in public in Washington. But I'd shock those men with my ideas too.

To Thine,
Alice

May 24, 1902
Diary—

So many things to tell! A few days ago, as I moped around the house because I hadn't a letter from Carpenter in ages, I wandered into a spat my father and stepmother were having about a French delegation's visit. Edith hasn't been well lately, and she didn't want to attend all of the tiresome engagements. As I loped into the room, my father stood up and said, "All right! Alice and I will go! Alice and I are Toughs!"

I was secretly very pleased, although I tried to act nonchalant in front of my parents. My father knows how much the French adore me, and how I return that feeling, and that in all honesty the delegation would probably rather dine with me than with Edith.

Early in the day we headed out to Annapolis with our French friends to see the ship Gaulois. It was a beautiful day, with a bright blue sky and hints of summer carried in the warm breeze, and getting out of Washington was refreshing and rejuvenating. Seeing the ship wasn't as thrilling as christening the Kaiser's yacht, but it was still fun to get on board. It reminded me of Cuba. I was a bit of a ham between photographs, but Father didn't seem to mind as I charmed the French with my antics.

We returned to Washington and went straight to the French Embassy for a formal dinner. And that, Diary, was delicious (perhaps my brother Archie is right to tease me about how much I eat—we've had quite a few brushes due to that topic). The cuisine wasn't really what piqued my interest, though. Sitting next to me was the most dashing, debonair Frenchman: Charles de Chambrun. He slyly flirted with me during the whole meal, and I shamelessly did the same. When I sneaked Emily out of my purse as a test for him, he giggled delightfully and seemed intrigued that I would carry a snake around with me. Our hands "accidentally" brushed on more than one occasion while we buttered our bread. Being in Charles's charming company wiped my mind clean of any traces of Carpenter, from whom I received a very angry, inflammatory letter recently. Seems he was mad that I danced a cotillion with some other boy. Well, he wasn't there for me to dance with, correct? He can't expect "Princess Alice" to stand alone at a ball.

Of course, I will see Edward again in only days. He will visit the White House on the twenty-seventh. Days ago I anticipated his arrival with such eagerness that I could barely sleep, but now I don't feel excited. My cousin Helen wrote me once joking, "How many little heartlets have you broken since I last heard from you?" I suppose I've learned the hard way that it's better to be the one who leaves first. Poor Carpenter, he will have to learn that bitter lesson on his own too.

To Thine Own Self Be True,
Alice

Chapter 10

Readjusting to school at Friends after my wonderful winter break wasn't too bad, although with my new schedule, I didn't have a single class with Quint and barely saw him. The Washington whirlwind, as usual, swept my parents away as soon as Air Force One touched down in DC. The real problem, however, was that my White House "Bye" was gone.

"Debra!" I bounded into the kitchen the first night I was home, expecting to see her baking up some goodies. Instead Maurice, one of the other chefs, stood in front of the range, stirring a soup pot. "Oh."

"Sorry to disappoint," he teased.

I blushed. "No offense—I was looking forward to seeing her. When is Debra working next?"

Maurice wiped his hands on a towel, frowning. "Probably not for a while. I have bad news—she's taken a leave of absence."

"What do you mean, 'a leave of absence'?"

"Her daughter is very sick. Debra went to Arizona to help take care of her grandkids." Maurice paused. "I'm not sure when she'll be coming back."

"Her daughter's sick? Like the flu?" I said hopefully.

Maurice shook his head and cleared his throat. "No, dear. She has cancer."

My hand shot up to cover my gasp. *Poor, poor Debra.* "That's horrible—I'm so sorry for her. Can I do anything to help?" The full importance of my dad's work hit me. *He needs to work that hard for families like Debra's.*

"You know, I could give you her email address," Maurice said. "I'm sure she'd love to hear from you."

"Definitely!"

Maurice put down his ladle and wiped his hands, then pulled out his phone. He scrolled through for a few seconds. "Kitchen grease really mucks up a touchscreen. Here it is. Ready?"

"Yeah." I pulled out a pen to write it on my hand.

"It's Secret-Agent-Chef, one word, at mail dot com." I smiled, wondering if the address was in response to my CIA confusion when Debra and I first met.

Maurice went back to cooking, and I sat down at the counter in shock. I felt terrible for Debra, and a little guilty—for taking up so much of her time when she could have been with her own daughter, and for selfishly thinking of how much her being gone would affect me. I caught a whiff of butter and lemons from whatever Maurice was making, and I felt a pang for Debra's soft voice and warm hugs.

Without Debra to confide in anymore, I read more and more of Alice's diary. Kind of obsessively. My breakthrough came from the entry in which she wrote, "Fill what's empty, empty what's full, and scratch where it itches." *Alice sought life out. She filled what was empty—she didn't wait around for someone else to make her feel better.* I wondered how Alice could rebound from bad things so quickly. In one entry, she was pining after Edward. In the next, she was so over him, making jokes about breaking his and other heartlets. I tend to sink into my loneliness and linger in it like a warm bath. *Maybe I need to live more like Alice.* I took a paint pen and wrote "WWAD" on an old bangle bracelet—*What Would Alice Do?*—to remind me to stop waiting to feel better, and fill what was empty. If "To Thine Own Self Be True" was Alice's motto, *WWAD* would be mine.

In my mopey state, I'd slacked on finding a way to get what I wanted—freedom to go on the school trip. Now more than ever, I needed to go so I would have time with Quint. I'd sort of exhausted my parents with pleas to attend already, so I decided to go to the only other person who could make New York happen for me, Denise Colbert. It was time to do what Alice would do: give Denise my very best elbow-in-the-soup treatment.

❧

I caught her in a hallway in the West Wing, just before six. "Hi, Denise," I said, smiling brightly. She nodded and waved, still hustling down the hallway in her sensible heels. I followed after her.

"Can I help you with anything?"

Denise raised an eyebrow. "Don't you have homework to do, Audrey? It's a school night."

"Finished it." I smiled again and batted my eyelashes at her. *I don't think I'm doing this right. This feels more like being flirty than persuasive, which is so wrong.* "I thought I could give you a hand. I'm really good at collating." That was true—in my mom's early campaign days, I spent hours collating papers for her campaign manager. I am also great at affixing stamps and checking off names on mailing lists.

Denise sighed but stopped moving. She absentmindedly tapped a pen on the file folder she was holding. "I suppose you could help me organize a few things in the file room. Make some copies. But, Audrey—you don't *have* to do any work. We have plenty of staff."

"I'd love to help! I find the work you all do around here fascinating, just truly incredible." I leaned toward her, my elbow resting on top of the file cabinets lining the hallway. It was a little high, so I had to stand on my tiptoes a bit so my hand could casually cup my forehead. I didn't exactly have a soup bowl to lean into.

"Okay." Denise gave me a weird look. "I'm going to pull a few files and ask you to make copies, then."

"Fantastic! Stunning!" I said, clapping my hands. I felt like an idiot, like I was troweling it on way too thick. Really, showing any enthusiasm for boring office tasks would be exaggerating. I followed Denise down the hall to a room with more file cabinets and a large copier.

Denise started pulling out files and handing pages to me. I stood next to her and held them in a neat stack. "So what are you working on lately?" I asked.

"Clean-energy initiatives, mostly."

I widened my eyes. "Tell me more!" *I feel like the only thing I'm convincing her of is that I'm a weirdo.*

Denise coughed. "We think that would be a good secondary platform for your dad to pick up. Given his science background."

"That's *very* interesting." I nodded and grinned. There was my chance. "I was thinking about a platform for myself, actually."

"Is that so?" Denise's eyebrows raised, and she stopped shuffling through the file she was holding. "Like what?"

"The arts, maybe?" Denise nodded, without a lot of enthusiasm. I continued anyway. "So my school has this spring trip to New York. I could go and see some performances, or go to a museum—it could be part of my platform. Getting kids interested in the arts."

Denise shook her head, her sleek hair swinging back and forth in front of her face. "You could go to a museum in DC; the National Gallery, maybe. But New York is out of the question." Denise straightened her hair and returned to flipping through the folder. "In the first place, I'm not sure how your mother feels about you doing your own public appearances." The little glimmer of hope I had faded. I felt crushed by her lack of interest, and a little insulted that my mom didn't think I could do my own appearances. *It's her fault, for never giving me a chance to prove myself.*

"Okay, I think that's enough for you to copy for now," Denise said. I had a fat stack of pages in my arms. "Give them to my assistant whenever you're done. Thanks for the help." With that, she spun on her heel and was out the door. I was left with a lot of photocopying to do and the sense that the elbow-in-the-soup treatment had failed me.

May 29, 1902
Diary—

I am going to have to ensure that no one ever finds this
diary because if some person does read this, and tells
my stepmother that I have been proposed to, it will
be "Off with her head!" for poor Alice. Yes, I am the
recipient of a marriage proposal. Actually, I received
two. It is quite a long story.

Two days ago, Edward Carpenter, formerly known
as my beau, currently known as a fool, arrived at the
White House. Sadly for Carpenter but (given the tumul-
tuous nature of our courtship) probably best for both of
us, Charles de Chambrun and a Knickerbocker gent in
my circle, J. Van Ness Philips, have already swept in and
swiped my interest from Edward. All four of us attended
a dinner, during which those three relatively handsome
young men all vied for my attention. (A scene straight
out of one of my wildest dreams.) We were seated far
down the table from my parents, so fortunately they
didn't overhear when Van Ness, after a bit too much
of the whiskey I had smuggled to the dinner inside my

long gloves, loudly turned to me and proposed marriage.
I hadn't imbibed the whiskey myself, but still I could not
control my laughter. Poor Carpenter appeared stricken,
slowly turning as red as the wheels of a steam fire engine
as it dawned on him that he had real competitors.

The next day Carpenter and I went for a long
walk in the gardens. He stammered and stuttered, and
it took him over two and a half hours to explain to me
how he felt about me. Poor Carpenter, I did love him
once upon a time, but now I can only see how twitchy
he gets when nervous, how his nose is actually slightly
crooked to the left (in addition to his woefully lopsided
smile), and how his Adam's apple pops out of his neck
in a most distracting and unappealing way. Recall that
letter he slipped me at dinner in Cuba? I no longer
think his admission that he "has nothing to say" is part
of a clever pun. It's close to an unfortunate truth. Yet
here are the points that he managed to sputter out:

–That he wishes to call me "Alice" when we are
alone together (not "Miss Roosevelt")

–That he is madly in love with me

–That he would like to marry me (Personally,
I feel that this was brought on more by the spirit of
competition more than anything else. I saw how he
used to look at Janet.)

I told him positively no. I told him that we were behaving like two idiots and that he could not possibly ask me to marry him. He tried to interrupt me and make his case again, but I wouldn't hear it. I bid him adieu and wished him well, but sternly. If he hadn't acted so idiotically, I might have felt remorse. But I didn't then, even if I feel a smidgen now.

I received notes this morning from both Carpenter and Van Ness. It's all very foolish of them. Of course at my age I am not in a position to accept their proposals, much as I might welcome the attention of a White House wedding and a husband to help me escape out into the world. Further, our society set has rules about these sorts of situations. Once a lady refuses a proposal of marriage, the man must accept it at once and refrain from asking again or otherwise pursuing her. To continue writing her, practically begging—it's simply not done. Those boys know that. For that reason, I really can't pity either of them.

Who would have thought earlier this spring, when my stepmother read that newspaper article about dueling suitors and got so angry at me, that the article was prescient? Certainly I didn't. I will do my very best to make sure that Edith never finds out about this little incident, and God forbid my father does. If they were upset about fictive multiple suitors, I imagine if I had to admit that two men really did propose to me within twenty-four hours, my parents would never, ever let me see the world outside my room again!

To Thine Own Self Be True,
Alice

June 7, 1902
Diary—

Alice is in big trouble, Diary dear. Thankfully, however, it's not because my stepmother found out about the proposals. Trouble started last week when Maggie and her Murad cigarettes came over. The scent of the "Turkish delights" must've wafted out of my room and across the hall to Edith's sitting room. All of a sudden my door burst open and Edith stormed inside, shrieking something about "being unladylike" and "filthy cigarettes." She snatched them right out of my hands and threw open the window. Then she called my father in from his office. Similarly displeased, he gave me a very blustery impromptu speech about how "no daughter of his would be smoking under his roof." I snidely pointed out that it wasn't actually his roof—it

belonged to the government and the American people
and he and I were temporary tenants—but that only
made him turn a redder shade and sputter. Finally, I
adopted a chastened expression and professed that I
would never smoke under his roof again.

Maggie was set to return home, but I gleefully
said, "Wait, Mags my dear—I am only allowed not to
smoke for one particular preposition regarding the roof
of the White House: under. Should I be smoking over,
around, through, on top of, adjacent to, etcetera,
I see no reason why that's breaking the statute."
Maggie's red-painted mouth curled into a grin. "How
do you suppose we get on top of it, then?"

All us kids like to climb out our windows down to
the grounds below, so I figured that from the attic level
it would be easy to climb out and go up. We hurried
up into the attic and opened the first window we came
across. I went first, being more limber than Maggie. I
swung myself out, grabbed the edge of an eave, and
had Maggie lean out and push as I pulled myself up.
Once I was entirely on the roof, I pulled her arms as
her legs kicked up the wall toward the roof. The roof
of the White House is flat, much like an unfinished
terrace, so there was little danger of us slipping and
sliding off into the shrubbery below.

We settled near to the edge and happily struck a match against some brick. However, one of the Secret Service men on the grounds happened to hear us laughing and looked up. Eventually my father and stepmother were called outside and stood, hands on hips, ordering us to come down immediately. (Well, Edith was wringing her hands.) Needless to say, another talking-to followed. It won't stop me from doing as I please, though. My parents ought not to be so controlling of me and so concerned with my "public image." Someone must teach them a lesson about letting a girl live her life!

To Thine Own Self Be True,
Alice

June 19, 1902
Diary—

I have escaped the melodrama surrounding Philips, de Chambrun, and Carpenter, and the repercussions of my little protest on the roof—by escaping to my beloved Chestnut Hill! I was so eager to get away that I packed my steamer trunk days in advance of the trip to Boston. My father teased me by asking if I was adopting President Harrison's view of the White House as a jail. I countered that actually, a jail hasn't got the same staggering number of rules. Or watchful eyes. Or snooping maids. I might've hurt Father's feelings.

Now that I am away, I do miss my siblings, and I suppose I miss my father and stepmother too. In some ways, I am able to feel more like a part of my family while I am missing them. It's normal to feel lonely when you are away from your loved ones, but it's queer to feel lonely while surrounded by family. That's often how I feel at home. Here in Boston I am rightfully the center of attention around my friends and my Lee relatives.

One wonderful thing about Chestnut Hill is that neither the press nor the Secret Service men trail me here. Those men have started paying more attention to my whereabouts in Washington—I suspect per Edith's request. It's really a bother to have them accompany me when I choose to walk into town to shop or go out for a dinner party. Lord knows I love how the reporters and photographers fawn over me, but there is a real freedom in being able to leave the house in Chestnut Hill without one of them around to extrapolate rumors from my choice of shoes or take a picture of me with mussed hair.

Last week, my friend Lila and I drove to one of the Pops concerts. We didn't go in my runabout but a larger automobile that Lila's father owns. How I love driving; I love the dusters one wears, I love the noises autos make, I love the freedom of traveling at the speed of a team of horses. Or more. I have gotten another speeding ticket.

I may have the funds to buy a fancier automobile because Grandpa Lee has agreed to raise my allowance. That's bully good! I will be able to shop madly and keep up with the likes of Lila here and Maggie back in Washington. You might think that because I am the First Daughter, I must not want for anything. It's true that I have received all manner of loot as gifts, from foreign dignitaries and my "fans" alike. But despite our pedigree, my family does not have the same wealth as many of my well-heeled friends, and I have spent through my allowance countless times already trying to keep up with them. It's hard for me, because I have to fill my role as "princess" and look fashionable and live lavishly. I am afraid of what people would say if the newspapers reported that I rewore an old garment. Edith and I have altered old dresses such that not even the sharpest newspaper columnist can keep track of what I'm wearing, which *is important. People love thinking of me as some kind of American royalty. If I stopped being glamorous and worthy of breathless newspaper stories, I worry I'd revert to plain, lonely, poor Alice.*

To Thine Own Self Be True,
Alice

The next weekend, practically the whole school headed off to Ashland to watch the Friends team kick butt at Science Olympiad. Quint was going, which I found out when I ran into him on my way into sixth period that Friday. Running into him in the halls was enough to make my *month*. The second I saw his dark curls from across the hallway, my heart started to do the hootchy-kootchy.

"Hey, Audrey!" he panted. He must've run down from his locker to catch me in the hallway. "How was Minnesota?" *Have we really not had a chance to talk since we got back from break?*

"It was awesome to be home." I smiled. "How was your break? Did you stay here?"

"No, my family always goes up to Vermont. Skiing and stuff."

"Sounds fun! I love skiing. Well, cross-country at least." Other students were rushing past us, so I inched a little closer to Quint to stay out of their way. He smiled at me and leaned in.

"Are you going to Ashland this weekend? For the Science Olympiad?" My heart sank. *Of course not.*

"No, I can't. Sadly. Why—are you?"

He nodded. "My buddy is on the team. It sucks that you can't go. I thought maybe you would because it's an official school thing or whatever." He shrugged. "Speaking of which—any word on the class trip? You're coming, right?"

"I'm…yes. I am totally going," I lied. *What am I thinking? I don't have permission yet.*

"That's great news!" Quint leaned in and gave me a half-hug. "I have to run to class. See you around?"

"Yeah, sure." *Although I have no idea where you'll see me other than right here in the hallway, unless you find a way to teleport yourself into 1600.* I lingered in the hallway, thinking about the stalled state of Operation Class Trip. I was out of ideas on how to convince people to give me permission. I felt the bracelet on my wrist and looked down at the letters *WWAD.* Alice Roosevelt would do whatever it took—even if that meant breaking all the rules. Maybe I would have to do that too.

On Saturday afternoon, 1600 was quieter than usual. Both my parents were on a trip to the West Coast, and they'd taken a lot of staffers with them. By midafternoon I was wandering the halls aimlessly, missing Debra. I poked around in the library, trying to find any pictures of Alice stored in there. I didn't find any originals, but one of the books about the Roosevelts had a picture of her standing next to a weird-looking car, and the caption said it was her "Red Devil." I smiled; I could picture Alice zipping around like a race-car driver, sort of a proto–Danica Patrick.

I'm still over two and a half years away from a license, even two years from getting my learner's permit. Not that it matters because if my mother is still president, there'll be no way on earth I'll get to start driving. It pissed me off, thinking about how the freedom of the road is another typical teenage freedom I won't get to taste. Harrison used to take me out in his sports car, and we'd drive down lonely country highways at incredible speeds. He promised to teach me how to drive when I got old enough. *But how will he do that if I'm in DC? Who knows when I'll get any closer to driving a car than driving a go-kart?* In fact, I can't even drive a go-kart anymore; the Secret Service deemed amusement parks high-risk locations for me.

Go-karts…remind me of golf carts. The White House has a slew of them, for staffers and security to zip around the property. The carts are another part of the green initiative because they're electric, and they charge with solar power. I took some training and now I'm actually allowed to operate them—with supervision. It's so random that they let me, considering the eleventy-billion rules and regulations I'm subject to as a Fido. I dropped the picture of Alice I was still holding and bolted out of the library.

Once outside in the court, I darted onto the lawn, which was free of snow thanks to a warm spell. I took a minute to gaze off at the Washington Monument and the Lincoln Memorial, way off in the distance. Then I scurried down the path, heading west toward one of the quieter security checkpoints. A guard sat inside, and a golf cart was parked next to the booth's door. The keys were dangling in the switch. *Seriously? They keep the keys* in *the carts? Although the rate of auto theft on White House grounds must be, uh, pretty low.*

I walked up to the door and knocked. The guard jumped a little in his seat, then reached over and pushed the door open for me. "Afternoon, Audrey. To what do I owe the pleasure?"

"I came out to get some air. I was wondering, could I take the cart for a spin?"

"Hmm, let me see if that's allowed today," he said, scratching his head. "Won't you get cold out there?" he asked as he scanned the daily security bulletin.

"I'm from Minnesota, remember?" I kidded. "This feels balmy to me."

He laughed. "Let me make a call." He grabbed his radio and started whispering in it. *"Tink wants to borrow a golf cart for a spin…Okay, away from the South Lawn fence. Not past the beehive. 10-4."* He turned back to me. "Good news! Shift supervisor said it's okay, so long as you stay on the South Lawn and don't go past the beehive."

"Thank you!" I raced over to the car and slid in through the open side. I hadn't driven one around the lawn in months, but golf carts are pretty self-explanatory. I paused to check and adjust my mirrors before starting the cart up. Then I turned the switch to ON and pressed the accelerator pedal. We started rolling. Painfully slowly—and backward. *Oops.* I pressed the brake and switched the drive switch from REV to FWD. Then I stomped down on the gas, and the cart lurched forward. I swerved immediately to avoid slamming into the side of the booth as I pulled away. "Are you sure you don't need a refresher?" the guard yelled after me. I pretended not to hear him.

Once I was past the swing set, I turned off the paved path and onto the lawn, heading past the fountain. The car sped up heading down a hill, although it couldn't go faster than fifteen miles an hour. "Red Devil, you are not," I laughed. There was enough speed that my hair was whipping around and the wind was freezing me—I was only wearing leggings and a Minnesota Golden Gophers sweatshirt—but I didn't care. The wind felt like freedom. It was laughing with me. Without planning it, I headed off toward the perimeter. I could see people on the other side of the fence, probably random tourists standing and taking their pictures. *How hilarious would it be for me to whiz past on my cart?* I giggled just thinking about it and pressed harder on the accelerator. Sure, they'd told me to stay behind the beehive, but whatever. *WWAD?*

When I got closer, though, I could see that they weren't tourists. It was a crowd of twenty to thirty people, holding signs and chanting.

"What do we want? Marriage equality! When do we want it? Now!"

The signs were covered with hand-drawn rainbows and statements like, *Equalize Love!* and *Marriage Is a Civil Right!* I screeched to a stop. What was I supposed to say to them? *Sorry, guys, I agree. But your cause isn't important enough for my mom to pay attention to right now.* I revved the engine to hightail it away from the fence and the protestors. *I need to turn back now, before they see me.*

Too late. "Hey!" someone shouted. "Tell your mom that we want our civil rights too!" The other people cheered. My stomach lurched, not just because I was slamming down the accelerator as I made a sweeping turn to head back. I kept stomping on the pedal, desperate to get away before the camera phones started coming out. The cart chugged over a soft hill as I took my hands off the wheel to brush my hair off my face. I glanced down at my wrist to see if I had a hair tie on it, but it was bare except for my *WWAD* bracelet. When I looked back up, I was headed straight for the Kitchen Garden at top golf-cart speed. I shrieked and frantically grabbed the wheel, starting to swerve. I narrowly missed the eggplant, but in doing so, I charged directly in the path of the papaya tree. I slammed on the brakes, but it was too late. The cart ran right into the tree, passenger-side first. It was barely going ten miles an hour, yet the whole front of the passenger side crunched on impact with the hard side of a plant bed next to the tree, and I slammed into the steering column. The jolt caused me to knock my elbow against the hard dash, and my arm ached immediately. I felt dizzy with panic. I switched to REV and tried to back up, but the cart was caught in the mulch and squashed plantings. I think I ran over a little decorative sign with a Thomas Jefferson quote on it, and it was stuck in one of the wheels. It wasn't going anywhere. *I am in such big, huge, massive trouble.* The wheels spun, and the engine made a scary whining noise. Shivering, I climbed out to abandon the cart and ran up the path toward the residence. I saw a duo of carts rolling toward me, filled with pairs of stern-faced security agents. And Denise Colbert. I groaned and clutched my arm. *This isn't going to be pretty.*

Chapter 12

And the aftermath of my accident *wasn't* pretty. First they rushed me to the White House doctor to make sure the crash hadn't injured me. "Mishap!" I insisted on calling it. *Crash* sounded way too melodramatic. My elbow was bruised and sore but otherwise fine, and as soon as I had my clean bill of health, I reported to Denise's office for a "chat."

For a few awkward minutes after I got there, I sat on the reddish leather chair in front of her imposing desk and had a staring contest. The pendulum of a large grandfather clock to the right of Denise's desk clicked back and forth like a metronome. The only photographs on Denise's desk are ones of her smiling tightly next to politicians. Denise lives and breathes White House politics. I don't think she has any kids, and I doubt she ever expected her role as Chief of Staff to include tasks like giving me a stern talking-to, so I felt a passing sympathy for her. Denise averted her eyes a few times to glance at some papers on her desk. The metronome clock kept its beat. Finally, she sighed, pushed the papers away, and spread her hands on the desktop. Her French-manicured nails were as meticulous as the rest of her. Denise struggled to maintain a neutral expression; a vein on her forehead was blowing her cover. "Audrey, would you like to explain to me what happened out there?"

Is that phrase in some kind of Dealing with Unruly Teenagers handbook? Any time I had a confrontation with an authority figure, they started by asking me to "explain" myself. It's annoying, particularly because the person usually thinks he or she already knows what happened, and has no interest in what I have to say about it. "Sure. I was driving a golf cart and, unfortunately, the papaya tree got in my way as I was headed back to return it." I shrugged and examined my cuticles intently. I didn't feel like attempting elbow-in-the-soup treatment with Denise again, and anyway my elbow hurt.

"I see. Weren't you told to stay away from the perimeter? To not go past the beehive?" Now her teeth were gritted in addition to the vein on her forehead tensing even further.

"I was so excited to be out driving that it slipped my mind." I fiddled with my *WWAD* bracelet.

"Audrey, let's get straight to the point." Pinch-faced Denise forced a fake smile. "*I* wouldn't have let you drive the cart in the first place. But although you had permission, you drove past the point you were told to stay behind. You encountered a protest, which was a *horrible* lapse in security. You proceeded to crash into the Kitchen Garden, damaging the cart and risking yourself injury. Now, I see a lot of problems with this." Speaking her mind seemed to relax Denise, but her tone made me slowly roll up out of my slouch and sit up straight. The cushion of the chair wheezed as I adjusted myself.

Denise continued, her voice rising, "This comes on the heels of your disrupting a State Dinner with an inappropriate dress. I understand you had a conversation with your parents about that. We all assumed that afterward, you understood the importance of your comportment. Although your temper tantrum at the school opening suggested otherwise."

The importance of your comportment. What was it with people like Denise and their insistence on using SAT vocabulary? I hate that.

"I made a mistake, but I wasn't in any danger, and I turned around right away. It's not my fault that people were out there protesting." I leaned toward Denise and narrowed my eyes. "Plus, I agree with them."

Denise stiffened. "That's where this becomes difficult, Audrey. I was once a teenager too." *No way! You mean you didn't come out of the womb at forty, wearing a skirt suit like that?* I kept the sarcasm in my head and nodded again. "I understand how this situation may be difficult for you, in terms of your personal freedoms. And your opinions." Denise paused, choosing her words carefully. "But you need to keep them to yourself. Particularly in public." My eyes widened. *Can Denise really do that? Tell me what I can and can't say? Or think?* "I've spoken to your mother and she agrees."

That was a blow. *How can my mom agree that I shouldn't have my own opinions? That's—she's being a hypocrite!* I didn't say anything.

"Audrey? Do you understand what we need you to do?"

"Sure." I refused to look her in the eye. "Can I go now?"

"Yes. And, Audrey—I *know* we won't have need for a conversation like this again." Her tone made it clear that was an order.

"Likewise." Because I didn't plan to take any more orders from Denise.

My bruised elbow turned a rainbow of colors overnight, so after my mom and dad returned I wore long sleeves at all times, even though the heat in 1600 had been cranked up to equatorial. I wasn't sure if Denise had said anything to them, but I definitely hadn't. My ever-distracted parents didn't find it weird that I was running around the Residence in thick Henleys paired with the shorts I usually wore over leotards. In their defense, they probably thought it was some silly new fashion trend, like wearing fuzzy winter boots with miniskirts or scarves with tank tops. At school I had no problem hiding my gross bruise, because the historic buildings on the Friends campus have crappy insulation and are perpetually chilly. Also, I think the uniforms were designed by the Pilgrims.

It got a little more difficult to hide Rainbow Bruise when my mom came up to my room Wednesday afternoon.

"What've you got planned for tonight?" she asked, still standing in the doorway. She was dressed up in her presidential best, so I could guess that my plans couldn't include her.

"Nothing," I said, sitting up and hiding my elbow behind my favorite lemon-patterned pillow. "Why?"

She grinned again, a smile like she was struggling to hide a very good secret. "Put on some clothes! Maybe your dance clothes."

I gave her a weird look, but got up and changed into some dance pants and a tank top while she waited outside. At the last second, I remembered to throw a hoodie on to hide my bruise. Mom waited patiently while I washed my face and brushed my teeth.

"Okay, I'm all dressed. Do I have somewhere to go? This is a school night, you know."

She smiled, sphinxlike. "Follow me," she said. "And grab a coat."

Mom refused to tell me where we were going in the car, and neither Hendrix nor Simpkins would give me any hints. But I figured it out as soon as we headed toward the Potomac and the lavender-lit Kennedy Center came into view.

"Seriously, Mom? Am I going to the Kennedy Center for something?"

She turned to me, grinning like a crazy person. "For a dance lesson!" She actually clapped with delight. "Your father and I wanted to surprise you with a fun perk, to make up for how busy we've been lately."

I squealed. "This is awesome!" I almost felt guilty about how angry I'd been at her lately, for not being around and for not letting me go on the New York trip.

"You'll get to watch the dress rehearsal of a performance, and then the dancers will give you a private lesson. Cool, huh? And if you like it, maybe we can arrange for more."

This is what I imagined life in the White House would be like. How many kids get to have private dance lessons at iconic performance spaces? "This is the coolest! And Denise doesn't care? There's going to be a lot of 'gyrating.' Her words, not mine."

Mom laughed. "Honey, Denise isn't the president. *I* am!"

June 22, 1902
Diary—

Well, I know not whether he is fit to handle my predilection for fine clothes and chocolates (and fine automobiles), but I have met the man of my dreams: Arthur Iselin.

Allow me to describe my love: he is tall and broad-shouldered and has a very dashing figure. His features are classic—a strong jaw and nose, and such full lips (not lopsided either). Arthur's eyes are dark and brooding, and he has lovely, chestnut-colored hair. As soon as I saw him at a dance a few weeks ago—the first time I had seen him in years—I was in love. Lila kidded that she would go and fetch her smelling salts for me, if need be.

You might think that this infatuation is silly, considering that I've been in his company only a few short weeks and rarely get a moment alone with him, away

from all of our friends and the requisite chaperones.
It's not, though, thanks to our intelligent and stimu-
lating correspondence. By pen he is the most charming
man I've met; in person he is infinitely more so. His
mind matches mine; it might even match my father's.
Arthur laughs at all of my silly jokes and outbursts,
and he told me that my "beautiful" eyes are worthy of
the thousands of dresses fashioned in their color.

Diary, I swear by all I believe in that if I receive
a third proposal, from Arthur Iselin, I would accept!

To Thine Own Self Be True,
Alice

July 2, 1902
Diary—

I am too angry for a long entry today. Four of my
girlfriends cornered me after dinner tonight and tried
to persuade me that I like Arthur too much. They had
the audacity to say that they were simply "trying to
open my eyes to his character." Well, I know Arthur's
character, and I love it. They might think that he is a
flirt, but they are wrong. They said that Arthur only
wants to get into the right political circles, but they are

jealous. I know Arthur loves me. He must love me. I can tell by how his dark eyes search out mine in every ballroom, dining room, or regatta we find ourselves both at. I simply won't listen to my friends—they must be envious of my good fortune in love.

Lila was not one of those traitorous girlfriends, but she and I are in hot water of another sort. You see, one of the papers reported that after attending a fancy dinner party, I was witnessed dancing with another young lady on the roof. Wearing only our undergarments. You can imagine how apoplectic Edith is—actually, I have to imagine it too, as I was informed of her displeasure through telegrams and a sternly worded letter. I've denied that said rendition of the hootchy-kootchy ever occurred, and I'm smart enough not to admit to it in these pages. Should I have danced in my underwear with Lila on the roof after a dinner party, well, I expect that we would have loved the rush from dancing unencumbered at a great height. We also would have loved the good spirits and cheers it would've evoked from our fellow partygoers down below us. I would also point out that, really, the types of undergarments good little Knickerbocker girls like us wear (the knickers we Knickerbockers wear! Ha!) are so binding and modest that we may as well have been wearing nuns' habits, and any ensuing controversy would be silly. If I were foolish enough to admit to doing that anyway.

Another thing annoying me at present is that one of my Lee uncles is intent on breaking me of my "scandalous" and "unladylike" smoking habit. I have the distinction of being the first woman in Washington to smoke in public. Not that many people could've seen me with a cigarette in hand, so I'm not sure how word has gotten around. Perhaps people know because I sometimes "accidentally" spill the contents of my purse at dinners, showing all the attendees the four things I always carry in it to parties: a strange, foreign fertility icon given to me in jest by a friend; a pocket copy of the Constitution; sweet Emily Spinach; and my taboo cigarettes. (No girl should be without those four items.) I don't know whether it's the garter snake or the cigarettes that shocks people more.

My point being—my uncle decided the best way to return me to Washington free of tobacco would be to sit me down and force me to smoke two big black cigars in a row. I suppose he thought my eyes would water, throat would burn, and it'd turn me off the stuff for life. Wrong! Although a cigar is a nasty thing to endure, I smoked both with feigned great enjoyment right in front of him, grinning broader as his face screwed up in frustration. When I finished, I licked my lips with gusto and asked him for a third. He snapped the box shut and stormed out of the room. (Thank heavens—I don't think I could have stood it!)

To Thine Own Self Be True,
Alice

Chapter 13

I was happy for days after my surprise Kennedy Center lesson. The dancers were amazing, and they were so patient when I was up onstage with them. My mom had even stayed for part of my lesson, and it reminded me of how she'd always take a break in her workday to pick me up from dance class in St. Paul. I always liked looking up and seeing her watching outside the rehearsal room. But my happy buzz faded when Madeline, Stacia, and Claire started passing notes back and forth in French later that week, and kept huddling deep in gossip before and after class. Occasionally, Madeline would shoot angry glances in the direction of Chris and me. *Something* was clearly up. On Friday, I found out what.

Madame Millepied broke the class up into conversation groups, and mine included Chris, Claire, and Stacia. When Madame left the room for a few minutes, their conversation work stopped and the gossip started.

"Chris, wasn't the party after Science Olympiad totally the best party of the year?" Stacia smirked as she said that, and I rolled my eyes.

"Yup." Chris Whitman: boy of few words.

"People were *really* celebrating our win," Claire insisted. She winked at Stacia and waited a beat before adding, "Madeline."

Chris perked up at that. "Huh?" Well, perked up for Chris.

Stacia glanced at Claire. She lowered her voice and half-whispered, "Madeline kissed someone." They paused to gauge Chris's reaction. He struggled to look like he didn't care. Finally, he asked, "Who?"

Claire cleared her throat. "That drummer guy she knows from band. I think his name is Quint. I have a picture of them together at the party." Claire held out her phone to Chris. I could see the screen as Chris held the phone at arm's length, like he was horrified by it. Perhaps *so* horrified that he was down from one word to zero. Madeline and Quint sat next to each other on a couch, so close their shoulders touched. Madeline was grinning. Quint was leaning down and toward her ear, like he was going to whisper—or kiss her cheek.

My hands went slack, and my pen fell to the floor, skittering to the side of my desk. I quickly bent down to grab it, pretending to have to search around to avoid having to sit back up right away. My heart was beating so fast I could hear it in my ears. I finally grabbed my pen and sat up again, red-faced. I hadn't heard what they'd been saying while I'd hung upside down. That was probably a good thing. My chest felt like it was going to explode. *If only I'd been allowed to go to Science Olympiad. I could've been sitting on that couch next to Quint.*

Claire said coyly to Chris, "We've probably said too much already." At that moment, Madame reentered the classroom. "I hope you've all been conversing in French this whole time, *non?*" A chorus of *oui* broke out in the room. I spent the rest of the class staring at Madeline with a mixture of anxiety, rage, and white-hot jealousy.

Just because the universe likes to mess with me, Quint was hanging around my locker after last period. He grinned as he saw me walking down the long hallway toward him, trailed a few doors back by Hendrix and Simpkins. I felt like punching a locker when I saw Quint's smiling face. He was looking at me so eagerly; he didn't have a freaking clue. *Were you smiling like that after you snuggled on the couch with Madeline last weekend?*

"Hey, Rhodes. What's up?" Clueless Quint moved aside to let me get into my locker. He had his drumsticks out and was *rat-tat-tatt*ing them on the adjacent locker to some tune only he could hear. I tensed my shoulders and stood perpendicular to him, spinning the dial of my lock with great concentration.

"Not much." I kept getting the combo wrong. "Jeez! Why doesn't this stupid school have fancy musical locks instead of these sticky, piece-of-crap ones?"

Quint took a step backward and pocketed his drumsticks. "Everything okay?" he asked tentatively. My locker finally popped open.

"Yeah, I'm fine…I guess *you* are too." I still didn't look him in the eyes. Quint frowned.

"Cryptic much?" Quint started drumming the adjacent locker again, with his fingertips. "What's that supposed to mean?"

I crossed my arms over my chest and finally turned to face him. "I don't know. What do *you* think it means?"

Quint rolled his eyes and swung his messenger bag over his shoulder. "I can take a hint. See you around." He turned and stalked away in the opposite direction from Simpkins. I shut my locker and leaned my forehead onto the cool metal door. *What am I doing? Crush or not, he's my friend. Singular.* Sighing, I pulled back and reopened the locker, distractedly shoving books into my backpack before giving it a cathartic slam.

After eating dinner alone, I wasted a few hours on Facebook, first checking all of the statuses of my old classmates in Minnesota, then seeing what the Friends kids were doing. I refreshed Quint's profile repeatedly, until a new status finally popped up. "Extra band practice." No question Madeline was going to be there too. I felt a lump in my throat and slammed my laptop shut.

I blasted some music and danced around my room, trying to get back to my post–Kennedy Center happy state until I collapsed in a sweaty heap on my bedspread. I wished I could escape to Debra's kitchen for some advice. I thought of Bye telling Alice that she could always come back to her when things got tough. My "Byes," Harrison and Debra, were both thousands of miles away. My dad was holed up in his 1600 lab space, way off in another wing. I could wander over there, but I knew from experience that if he was in the middle of data mode I could walk in bleeding profusely or with green hair or on stilts and he wouldn't bat an eye. My mom was off on another trip overseas, this time to India. I hated how she went to faraway places all the time, and I worried about her being on a plane so much. I feel so much more secure when she is just over in the West Wing, even if I see her *almost* the same amount whether she's in DC or Davos. Surprise dance lessons notwithstanding.

My arm trailed off the edge of the bed and pointed toward my desk drawer, reminding me what was hidden inside. *Alice had to deal with competition, that lovely Janet in Cuba. Maybe she'll show me how to one-up Madeline. Or, if that doesn't work, how to deal with a broken heart.* Alice seemed to spend a lot of time pining for guys, after all. I jumped off the bed and pulled open the drawer, fishing around until I felt the crumbly leather spine meet my hand. I pulled out the diary and opened it to the page I'd marked with the vintage postcard and started to read.

July 26, 1902
Diary—

I think my dear friend Lila wanted to distract me from my obsession with Iselin, so she suggested that I join her in Newport. I gladly went—Newport, the summer destination for the wealthy. My jaw permanently dropped at the opulent mansions. They put my family's home at Oyster Bay to shame; Sagamore looks like a shabby groundskeeper's cottage by comparison.

I became tired of mingling with society after a few days. It's always in such situations that I think of how Edith and I refashion my old dresses, and then I start to itch. Isn't it off that the daughter of the president can still feel pangs of inferiority? Power and wealth are not really the same thing.

Dying to get back to Boston, where Arthur was, I begged Lila day and night to bid adieu to Newport. Finally, she conceded—but on the condition that we take off by ourselves, with no chaperone. I, of course, thought that was the most genius suggestion I'd ever heard. Two bold and rebellious young ladies, taking off in an automobile by themselves and driving all the way from Newport to Boston. I've never driven that far without a chaperone.

We decided it would be best to leave at dawn to avoid having some stick-in-the-mud stop us "for propriety's sake." I'd hastily packed my hatbox and trunk the night before, so as soon as the sun started to creep over the horizon, I slipped out of my room and met Lila in the hall. We got to the automobile without being noticed but had forgotten how incredibly noisy they are to start. I thought I saw some window shades snapping up as the car sputtered and gagged to get going. We laughed gaily as we readied ourselves in the vehicle and took off down the bumpy lane. I never looked back, so I don't know if by that point anyone was watching us. I can picture the lady of the house running frantically into the drive, still in her dressing gown and slippers.

Getting back to Boston took most of the day. Lila and I took turns driving—I drove much faster than she did, of course. Every time we passed an intersection with another road, I honked the horn madly. We stopped along the road at lunchtime and ate a few roast-beef sandwiches that Lila had sneakily packed in the kitchen the night before, taking long swigs of water out of her canteen. We were covered in so much dust from the road that my white duster was completely black. My face and hair were darkened with soot too—except for two large circles around my eyes where the goggles had been. What a sight we were.

When we finally arrived in Boston, tired but exhilarated, Mrs. Paul was waiting at Lila's home, absolutely livid. She shrieked about how terrible and scandalous we'd been, and about how unsafe it was for us to take off on a long car trip. I put on my sweetest face and replied, "But it's terribly difficult to have such bully fun when a chaperone is present, Mrs. Paul." She retaliated by sending a telegram to my parents.

Now that I am back in Boston, I have heard from my father by letter about how "disappointed" he is that I chose to go for a spontaneous trip by automobile. Sometimes I wonder, though, if the man who led the Rough Riders in Cuba and tamed parts of the West is really that put out when his daughter does something unladylike. Yes, certain types of toughness are not

*considered proper for a woman, but I can't help it that
I, like my father, am a Tough. He's said so himself.
Sometimes I hope that although he chastises me when
I do something outrageous, part of him is proud of my
spirit. If not, that's just another abandonment of Alice
on his part.*

To Thine Own Self Be True,
Alice

August 4, 1902
Diary —

*The summer is winding down, and I am back in
Washington. It's strange to come home to a house full
of young children after such a long stint in polite society. (Not that my friends and I are always so polite.) I
was ambushed walking into the East Room yesterday
by the little ones. Quentin pelted me with his toy gun
and then Archie came in and beat me with a cushion.
I almost got angry toward them until I remembered
the fun I used to have doing the same with them. So I
got down on my hands and knees and hid behind the
furniture with them, waiting for some poor unsuspect-
ing staff to wander through and get assailed. Ethel*

wandered in and Archie hit her square in the face with a throw pillow.

Can you believe that my stepmother is still in the midst of renovations? It's now been a year since our family found our way into the White House. I long to live in a place that is neat and settled and not constantly being disrupted and changed, even if the renovations were sorely needed. If my father doesn't win the next election, we may never enjoy the fruits of Edith's labor.

What is making me melancholy about being back home is Arthur. I suspect that he holds little affection for poor me. At the last party we both attended, he barely spoke to me and spent the whole evening swooning over a beautiful Southern girl. I heard that he was disappointed that associating with me hadn't meant more to his prospects. Oh, I hate that I am so plain and unlovable! If I weren't, he might still care for me.

All I can think of these days, as I sit in my room and listen to the noise of children playing, renovations, and staff and visitors constantly tramping through the halls, is whether I shall ever dance with Arthur again. If he will ever again take my hand. If I should ever be able to kiss his handsome lips. My friends tried to warn *me that he was fickle, but I couldn't listen. One can't control whom her heart chooses to love, and mine has chosen to love Arthur. I simply wish his would love me for me.*

To Thine Own Self Be True,
Alice

Chapter 14

Alice must've been concerned about her maid snooping when she wrote those entries because her handwriting was almost impossible to read. Staring at the cramped letters gave me a headache, but soaking up her words was like guzzling an energy drink. I grabbed a school notebook and scribbled down the last lines of one entry: *"One can't control whom her heart chooses to love, and mine has chosen to love Arthur. I simply wish his would love me for me."* I felt the same way about Quint. I couldn't help my crush on him, and I just wanted him to like me back, Fido or not. It was like Alice, across space and time, knew exactly the words I needed to hear.

It was late, but I felt restless. I flipped back through, stopping on the entry where Alice and Maggie Cassini smoked on 1600's roof. *I suppose Alice didn't know how bad smoking is for you.* For her, smoking was a way to break the suffocating rules. I drummed my fingertips on the headboard. *I wish I had more ways to do that.* Living vicariously through Alice didn't feel like nearly enough. I thought more about how my mom and Denise didn't want me to have a platform, didn't want me to travel—they didn't seem to want me to be *me*, at least not in public. Highly controlled visits to the Kennedy Center and the like, while very cool, amounted to an ounce of freedom—not enough to feel like I was eating things up, Alice-style. *If I want freedom, I have to* take *it.* I hopped off my bed and walked over the creaky floor to my box closet. I kneeled down and reached behind a box, pulling out the handkerchief with the cigarettes still wrapped up inside. A smile crept across my face.

I dusted off the never-opened pack and reexamined the writing. "Murad Cigarettes." A mystery brand. "The finest Turkish tobacco leaf." There was a color drawing of an elegant woman wearing scarves and a turban in between the title and the tagline. She looked like she could be a hootchy-kootchy dancer. The box had no FDA or Surgeon General warnings. I sniffed at them, wondering if cigarettes spoiled. Obviously, these were from when Alice lived in the White House, and that was…more than a hundred years ago. I put the kerchief back in its hiding place, but took the cigarettes with me as I walked back to my desk.

I tapped the pack against my desk absentmindedly as I started googling "do cigarettes go bad" and "cigarettes get old" and "cigarettes rotten," but all I found out was that after they've been opened, they go stale. Well, this pack was *un*opened, although at least a century old. Nothing said ancient cigarettes get any more toxic than they usually are, or go rancid or whatever. Everything reiterated that they are terrible for you.

I'd never wanted to smoke before. Harrison is the only smoker I know. My mother has begged him to quit for years, to which he usually replies that he'll quit on his wedding day. Same-sex marriage still isn't legal where he lives, so Harrison is still a smoker. But honestly, he's tried and struggled to quit over the years, which really upsets my mom. What I knew about cigarettes: they're horribly addictive, they're gross-smelling, they're expensive. Not to mention totally illegal for someone my age. Still, I thought about teenage Alice smoking—puffing away on these very cigarettes—and what a rebel that made her. I wanted a taste of *her* type of freedom. *One or two cigarettes won't kill me. Right?* I felt a twinge of guilt, thinking of Debra's daughter and my dad's research, but I pushed those thoughts out of my head and pictured Alice instead. Sitting on the White House roof with her Murads.

I pulled on a black hoodie—for camouflage—and shoved my feet into a worn pair of fuzzy boots. I rummaged around in my desk drawer for the matches I kept for candles. I and the little box of the good wooden kind, from a favorite restaurant in St. Paul. I tucked them and Alice's cigarettes into my hoodie pocket and quietly slipped out the door.

I crept up the stairs to the third floor, where I hurried along the center hall to the Solarium. I assumed that when Alice wrote that she smoked on the "roof" of the White House, she meant she was up on the Promenade. It was during Alice's stepmom's renovations that they added guest rooms to what had been the attic level. Now the third floor is partly Residence living space and partly the patiolike Promenade. The Promenade is raised three feet higher than the rest of the third floor (except for the Solarium, where you can get onto it) and hidden from public view by a staunch balustrade. I'm definitely not allowed up there at night, but the door in the Solarium doesn't have an alarm or anything, so no one should know if I ventured outside. I unlatched the glass door and stepped out, shivering, in the moonlight.

Rather than stand on the rounded part of the Promenade, above the Truman Balcony, I walked past the windows of the game room and stood at the corner of the patio, outside some rarely used offices. There I pulled Alice's cigarettes and my matches out of my pocket. I peeled open the warped box and shook out one cigarette. It looked strange—not bleached white, like the cigarettes you see in the movies and magazine ads, but a mottled brown-gray. It wasn't perfectly shaped either, but a little lumpy. I sniffed it. It smelled like regular tobacco, but faintly. I put one end between my lips and held it there. It felt strange, kind of like the stick end of a lollipop, but more papery. Already, my stomach started flip-flopping and I felt a little sick. The balustrade barely protected me from the sharp wind; my hands were getting cold and stiff. *I'm guessing Alice only came out here to smoke in the summertime.*

I reached in my pocket to pull out a match, but stopped before my fingertips reached the box. *This is wrong. Superwrong. Epic-fail wrong.* On a lot of levels, and even *just-one-cigarette*, because I was certainly not old enough to smoke, and because these weren't any old cancer sticks. They were *Alice's*, and they'd been hidden in the White House for a century. They probably could be considered a historical artifact and should be in the Smithsonian or something— like her secret diary.

It was one thing to keep the diary for myself (for now, while I was reading it) and another to smoke her historical artifact. I'd probably done enough damage by opening the box and touching them. I could stop now and salvage them—*and* stay a nonsmoker. Did I really want to become a kid who had smoked? That was something I couldn't undo, and the more I thought about it, being tobacco-free *was* important to me. Awesome as Alice was, maybe not all of her shenanigans were worth repeating. She didn't know in 1902 how bad the Murads were for her. I bet if she had, she would've found another way to shock people. You can't exactly eat up a lot of life with emphysema.

I fumbled with my frozen fingers to put the cigarette back in the box, then slid down the wall to sit cross-legged next to the building, more sheltered from the wind. I *could* still hang out on the roof like Alice had. I sat and stared at the Washington night sky, contemplating how quiet 1600 was at night, how private. And cold. I could see my breath in front of me, like smoke, and that made me feel close enough to Alice. I set the Murad box on the Promenade floor beside me. I think Alice would've been proud that I was to *mine own self* being true.

While I sat, I thought about the trip. Maybe I'd never get permission. Maybe I'd need to go without it. *Alice didn't ask for permission to leave Newport and drive to Boston.* I'd have to start thinking of how I could ditch my agents and sneak along with the group. I vaguely remembered reading that the Bush twins used to escape their detail. I'd have to research to find out how.

I kept tapping my feet to stay warm. As I was reaching into my other pocket to grab some balm for my now-chapped lips, I heard the door to the Solarium burst open and someone come running out. I scrambled to my feet and peered around the corner. Simpkins. Alone, but with his walkie-talkie at his lips. *I'm totally not supposed to be here—I need to sneak back in before he sees me.* In the opposite direction of Simpkins, I dashed toward some stairs leading up to the Center Hall fire exit. If the door was unlocked from the outside, I could escape back inside, easy peasy. I ran up the short staircase and searched the stainless steel around the fire door for a button, any kind of button. Nothing. Now I was blocked from an exit except from running back, and possibly into Simpkins's path. I turned around and hurried toward the Solarium. Maybe he ran the other way and I could slip in unnoticed.

Seconds later, a tall figure rounded the corner and planted himself directly in my path. "Stop!" Simpkins's left hand was up like a crossing guard—and his right, terrifyingly, hovered near his holster.

"Don't shoot me!" I shrieked. I hunched down and shielded my face with crossed forearms, then peered through them to see Simpkins in front of me. Thankfully, with his gun still in its holster. "Audrey Rhodes." His gruff voice sounded bewildered. "What is going on here?" He pulled his crackling walkie-talkie up to his mouth. "All clear. Situation under control. Tink accounted for." He paused. "No, no backup needed. She was outside. False alarm."

Shakily, I stood up. "I...needed some air." I shoved

my trembling hands into my pockets—and felt only the matches. *Crap!* Where had I left those cigarettes?

Simpkins saw me shivering. "I think we can take this discussion inside." I nodded, and we headed for the door.

Once inside, Simpkins sat me down for a talk. "Audrey, sneaking out of the house...I understand it was inside-outside, but the Promenade is off-limits at night. You could've gotten hurt. I only came out because we noticed a shadow on the security camera, and I suspected it might be you. But if someone else had been on duty..." I winced, thinking of the holster his right hand had been dangerously close to and what could've happened if I startled someone.

"I get it," I said, without a hint of petulance.

Simpkins smiled at me. "Can I trust you not to do it again?"

"You can. I *promise*," I said. And I meant it—that was as close to smoking on the roof as I ever cared to get.

Chapter 15

That Sunday, knocking on my door woke me up at 8:00 a.m.—way earlier than I usually get up. And everybody at 1600 knows that. Groggily, I pulled back my blankets and shuffled over to the door. "Yeah?" I opened it and saw my dad standing in front of me. With a worried, slightly mad look on his face. He stormed in, clutching the front section of a newspaper. I had no idea what I'd done wrong, but my stomach still dropped. "Um," I started.

"We need to talk," Dad said. He took one hand off the newspaper to rub the bridge of his nose.

"I figured."

Bad word choice. "This is *serious*, Audrey," he said, wearily. "Do you know what's in the paper today?"

"News?" Grogginess had morphed into crankiness. *How could this have anything to do with me?*

"I'm going to advise you to cut the lippiness." He dramatically cracked the paper open. "There's a story in the gossip section about *you*. It's been…enlightening." *How can there be gossip about someone who doesn't have a life?* This wasn't the first time the papers had reported supposedly private stuff about my family, from some jerk face "unnamed source," but it was the first time it was about *me*.

Dad continued, "I'll read it for you." He cleared his throat. "Our White House spies say that naughtiness abounds in the Rhodes residence. It seems the little First Lady is growing up—into a first-rate troublemaker." His voice unconsciously shifted to a snarky gossip tone as he read the copy. Under different circumstances, I would've cracked up. "She's been dressing for State Dinners like she's going to a club, pulling temper tantrums at school openings, and taking joyrides on White House grounds and crashing cars. As if Madam President didn't have her hands full enough with those low approval ratings. I guess it's time for the First Gent to step up? Where is he anyway? It's a mess at 1600 Pennsylvania…" Hearing "taking joyrides on White House grounds and crashing cars" made my heart stop. My parents didn't know about that. Or they *hadn't*.

"I didn't take a joyride and crash a car!" I exclaimed. "They got that wrong!"

"But did you take a golf cart to see a protest next to the lawn and crash it into the eggplant?" *Papaya tree*, I muttered, but he didn't hear me.

"I had permission to do that! Not to run into the kitchen garden, but to take the cart for a spin."

"And now look what someone found on the Promenade. After you were out there last night." He held out Alice's cigarettes, which I'd meant to hunt for in the morning light. "Were you smoking?"

"No!" I stepped backward and put out both hands as if to show I was clean. "Count them if you want—I didn't smoke any. I *swear*." I shook my head. The last thing I needed was to go on an unnecessary substance-abuse watch. "I found them in a closet—I think they were Alice's, I mean—*artifacts*."

My dad did stop to study the pack for a few minutes, turning it over in his palm. He opened it and saw that not a cigarette was missing. "That doesn't explain why you took a pack outside with you," he snorted.

"That's none of your business," I shot back.

"Not my business? Are you serious? I'm your father!"

"Then act like it!" My ears rang with the silence after that. I felt almost relieved, though—like maybe now we would finally talk about how he'd been slacking at being a dad. And how hurt I was by that. "Put away your laptop and your phone, and act like it," I said, a little louder this time.

For a moment, he stared at me. I don't think either of us could believe I actually said that. "I...I *am*. I have to, because...your actions have created a *situation*!" He stopped

199

and turned, hearing someone come up the stairs. In walked my jet-lagged, exhausted-looking mother—back from India. For once, she didn't seem presidential as she walked down the hallway. Her light-blue blouse was wrinkled and untucked, and she'd taken off her shoes somewhere and was walking in stocking feet. Her hair had lost its volume, and whatever makeup she'd put on before the long flight back had faded. She looked like my normal mom—but tired and frustrated.

Mom turned to me. "I'm going to try so hard right now to not blow up at you, Audrey Lee." That was a bad sign—she only calls me "Audrey Lee" when she's seriously mad. "What is going on with you? Do you know how serious this is, and how much damage control we're going to have to do? All I'm going to hear for days is"—she mimicked a nagging voice—"'How can she lead the country if she can't even control her kid?' 'How can she lead when even her daughter wants to protest?'" Her voice broke a little. "All this, and after Denise and I pulled those strings last week to treat you with a dance lesson?" She shook her head. "Cigarettes on the roof? I want to know what happened to my sweet girl."

"Helen, wait," my dad started to say.

My mom's words stung. *This is so unfair—I did the right thing on Friday night, even, and I'm still getting into trouble for it.* I clenched my fists at my side. "You want to know what happened? *You* happened. *You* had to run for president and *you* had to screw up all of our lives and *you* had to make me move here. *I* want to know what happened to my *mother*. Who is the *most* selfish person in this family."

"Audrey, don't speak to your mother like that!"

"Fine!" I shouted. "Madam President." My voice dripped with sarcasm. "I regret to inform you that it's your fault for running for president and ruining your daughter's life in the process." I raised my eyebrows and smirked.

My mom looked like she was either going to throttle me or cry. "That's it. You're grounded."

"Ooooooh. Grounding me. As if I'm not already living in a federal prison."

"Audrey, in your room. This discussion is over." My mom gestured toward the newspaper, which was sitting on my desk—on top of Alice's cigarettes, which my dad seemed to have forgotten about. I was relieved he hadn't thrown them out. "We have to go clean up this mess now." They stomped out of my room. As soon as my dad shut the door, I crumpled down onto my shaggy rug. I instantly regretted 75 percent of what I'd just said. I mean, yelled. Obviously I know my parents are good people trying to do great things. But it was like everything I'd been feeling since the campaign came spewing out of me during that fight, and I couldn't stop to think about what I was saying, and now I'd made a big mess into a huge hot one.

❧

September 5, 1902
Diary—

I'm writing in a somber state. Two days ago something terrible happened, and it has shaken me to my core.

My father was away in Massachusetts, and while riding in an electric trolley car, they were hit by a carriage. One of the Secret Service guards with him, dear William Craig, was killed. The children and I were all so fond of him. So was our father, who was fortunate to escape with mostly superficial cuts and bruises. Losing a good man like Craig is a tragedy, but one that could have been much worse. Only a year ago, on September 6th, President McKinley was shot and killed. That incident changed everything—it's the reason why the president has these brave Secret Service men to protect him. I shudder to think that another American president could have been lost with this fatal incident.

Things between my father and I have never been easy. How many times have I reflected on my father saying that he can be president of the United States, or he can control me, but he cannot possibly do both? Sure, I laughed upon hearing his quip, but truth is afterward I slunk out of the room and back upstairs, red-faced.

I love my father, and I believe that he is an exemplary person and great leader and politician. I want to make him proud; I do want his approval; most of all I want his love. Perhaps sometimes, when I'm all mixed up in my melancholic love for Arthur Iselin or busy wreaking havoc in polite society with Emily Spinach, I lose sight of that aim and don't really think about my actions.

Hence the past two days, I have gotten out of bed early like the rest of the family. The first day I padded down the stairs to the kitchen and joined them at the breakfast table; their wide eyes couldn't hide their shock. I'd rejected the family breakfast, long a Roosevelt tradition, since before we moved into the White House. I shook off their stares and took my place at the table, stirring cream into my coffee with my head down, and when I looked up, I saw a tired smile on my father's bruised and bandaged face. It was hard to tamp down the lump rising in my throat, but Alice is a "Tough."

I think I will keep meeting with my family at breakfast time, even if that means doing some of my nighttime reading during the day. I might complain about Edith, but I do think she loves me as much as a stepmother can and should and maybe a little more. I love Ted and Kermit and Ethel and Archie and little Quentin. The quiet moments in the morning with them (well, as quiet as breakfast for a family of eight can be) ground me, give me some perspective during the rest of the day when I am presented with fickle Iselin or another false report of my engagement.

I am so thankful that my father is safe and that September this year will not bring another presidential death to the White House. I pray for the family of William Craig, and we will all miss him so.

To Thine Own Self Be True,
Alice

September 25, 1902
Diary—

I have been busy lately, helping my father recover from a medical procedure related to the accident. Sitting around and helping him recuperate, I've allowed him to talk ideas and politics with me for long stretches of time. I surprised myself when I found what he had to say about politics interesting, for once. Some things we agree on, and some we do not. For example, I am accepting of homosexual love. I've said so many times at parties—my favorite quote on the matter is that I don't care what anyone's proclivities are, so long as he or she doesn't "do it in the street and frighten the horses." I repeated that idea enough in conversation that word got around, and I actually received a letter inviting me to become the first "honorary homosexual." What a newfangled idea! I adore it. I was going to show Father the invitation—jokingly tell him that I've earned their votes for him—but when I brought up the subject, I realized very quickly that our opinions could not be more in opposition. I kept the letter to myself, perhaps wisely, because Father has very traditional ideas on the subject.

But here's something we did agree on. Father's still consumed by the coal strike. The miners in Pennsylvania haven't backed down and neither have the owners, and my father is wrestling with the idea of whether he (i.e., the government) should do something about it. Now it's not only the unions and the coal company who will be affected; winter looms for the East Coast, and if the strike goes on, people won't have coal to heat their homes. It could be a chilly winter for this country if someone doesn't sort this out in a way that is fair to both parties. I think it is time indeed for the government to do something about an issue that concerns so very many people. Father has set up a fact-finding commission to find a way for both sides to end the conflict. At times like these, I feel so proud of him. In his words, he will lead them all to a "square deal" for both parties. Father was quite pleased with my interest in the subject. My parents keep telling me that I need to take up interests "outside myself." I can practically hear them thinking, Why can't Alice be more like her cousin Eleanor? So serious and studious and engaged in charity works with the Junior League. In my defense, I have made public appearances for the sake of charity. I've simply made many more for parties and balls.

Lest you think I am turning angelic, when I haven't been by my father's side, I have been reading up on draw poker and dice throwing. I really wet my whistle for gambling in Cuba. Some friends of mine and I have little secret poker games after dinner, and I am bleeding them all dry with my winnings. Gambling on an actual race or game is my favorite, but poker and dice are the surest ways for me to amuse myself lately. I've told Maggie about my betting history and made her *jealous. She's never gambled apart from poker playing, so I'm tutoring her in what little I know. One of these days, we'll escape to the Benning racetrack and make a mint. I have to admit that any time society labels an activity "unacceptable" for women, my interest in doing it, well and often, increases significantly.*

To Thine Own Self Be True,
Alice

October 15, 1902
Diary—

It is the wee hours of the night and I am still awake, sitting in my bed surrounded by books, unable to sleep but too agitated to read. I got a letter from a friend today and read all about how Arthur was seen flirting with some other girl. I suppose I was right, and the lion's share of his infatuation was with the novelty of my unique position as First Daughter. People always comment about what a charmed life I must lead because of that, but here's a confession, Diary: It's horrible at moments like this. I feel so foolish for believing that Arthur had eyes for me. Or for me only, I suppose. Compared to my friends, I am nothing. The countess and the belle, Maggie and Lila, are so attractive and bright and everyone likes them so much. They don't need titles like I do. It's hard to have beautiful friends like them while being a perfectly nondescript sort of person, physically.

Now I am so miserable, living in a world without Arthur's affection. After all this heartsickness, I doubt I will ever marry. I don't want to be abandoned by anyone else in my life; Tough or not I can't bear it. So I'll be a fabulous old maid. I'll host parties for rich, powerful, and brilliant guests and be a Washington Grande Dame—on my own. Perhaps I'm lucky to be the child of a successful politician because I don't need a husband to gain entrance to these spheres of society. Bully for me.

To cheer myself up, I think I will scrounge up some friends for a day at the races. Maggie will surely be game. Technically, there's no harm in us attending Benning racetrack; it's the betting that rankles the fuddy-duddies. I must ensure that no one (particularly those wily reporters) sees me exchanging money for a bet. The racetrack will be good medicine for my melancholy. Nothing lifts my spirits like earning some greenbacks through gambling.

To Thine Own Self Be True,
Alice

My mom's a firm believer in never going to bed angry: at her spouse, at her kid, at her constituents, probably. Getting to the White House upended that rule. By Sunday night, my parents and I still weren't speaking. I hid out in my room, not wanting to be the one to break the standoff with my parents; I felt too right to apologize but too jerkish to act like I hadn't said horrible things to them. Even though my stomach was being scarily vocal, no way was I going to venture out. *They* were going to have to come to *me* and extend the olive branch. Thank goodness for the cookies I kept stashed in my desk drawer, otherwise I would've starved.

My trusty First Friend laptop kept me company. I opened chat and saw my list was sparsely populated, except for one name with a bright green dot next to it: Quint. Instinctively I smoothed my hair and sat up straighter. Which was silly because: (1) video chat doesn't work with the firewall, and (2) we weren't exactly speaking either. I was on a roll—the only people not currently pissed at me were Kim and Harrison. Both oh-so-conveniently located 1,098 and 847 miles away, respectively.

I stared at Quint's name, willing him to IM me. I tapped out a pithy status ("Me, myself, and I—won't you join us?"), then decided it was stupid and deleted it. I changed my icon from available-green to busy-red. I scrolled through my photos and uploaded a cuter one (of me laughing in a non-fake way) for my profile image. I switched back to available-green. I opened another tab for my email, but kept checking back to see if Quint was still there. He was. I wondered if he was busy talking to Madeline. That made me feel a little sick.

Only when I got distracted by finally starting an email to Debra did I hear the ping of a new message. I clicked back, crossing my left-hand fingers that it was Quint. And it was.

DrummerBoy: You there, Audrey?

tinydancer: Yeah.

DrummerBoy: What's up?

tinydancer: Not much. What's up w/ you?

DrummerBoy: Studying. I don't get this mitochondria stuff.

tinydancer: What's not to get? It's in cells, and it makes energy.

DrummerBoy: Says the MacArthur Genius's kid.

tinydancer: He doesn't have a MacArthur.

DrummerBoy: Touché.

tinydancer: Anyway, I don't think he'll be helping me with my homework anytime soon.

DrummerBoy: ????

tinydancer: Big fight.

DrummerBoy: Pourquoi?

tinydancer: Well…it's a long story. I got caught doing something I shouldn't have been doing.

DrummerBoy: I do read the news, ya know.

tinydancer: Oh. Yeah. That stuff.

DrummerBoy: South Lawn joyride? That's so bada$$, Audrey.

tinydancer: There was more to it than that. I mean, I had permission to use the cart, and the crash was an accident. And what do people expect me to do with my time anyway? I'm stuck in the WH and usually alone.

tinydancer: Anyway, I am in deep shizz.

DrummerBoy: Sorry to hear it. You okay? Re: parents?

tinydancer: It's never fun to be told how disappointing you are.

DrummerBoy: I'm sure they don't mean it like that. It'd be impossible for you to be a disappointment.

tinydancer: Thanks.

tinydancer: I kind of needed to hear that from some-one tonight.

DrummerBoy: My pleasure.

DrummerBoy: If it makes you feel better, mine are always on me about spending too much time practicing drumming and too little studying history or foreign languages.

tinydancer: Oh, the struggles of a diplomat's kid.

DrummerBoy: Or the president's kid.

tinydancer: Maybe just of being a kid with Very Important Parents.

DrummerBoy: You got it.

tinydancer: Totes.

tinydancer: I should probably go get ready for bed. School night.

DrummerBoy: Ditto. Maybe I'll see you around this week?

tinydancer: Yeah, sure.

DrummerBoy: G'night.

tinydancer: Night.

I was smiling so hard that I took a picture with my webcam. I wanted to document how superhappy I looked.

My crush on Quint was growing exponentially, like

those Fibonacci bunnies. I was about 96.4 percent sure that he had a crush on me too—at least he flirted with me a lot. *What does it mean, though, if Quint is already in the middle of something with Madeline?* It was confusing. *And how could a girl living in 1600 today ever have a boyfriend?* Alice had Carpenter and Arthur and all those guys fawning all over her at fancy dinners. But she also got to ride her bike on the streets of Washington and travel and basically *live*. I wanted something to happen with Quint, but I was afraid that trying to go from being friends with him to *more-than-friends* could lead only to more loneliness. I looked down at my *WWAD* bracelet. Even though I got the impression *any* guy could fall in love with Alice, her dating successes gave me a smidgen of hope. Maybe I needed to fill what was empty. To mine own self be true, and mine own self was pining for Quint. Maybe, if I wanted something to happen with him, I would have to make 1600 work for me, instead of against me, for once. The White House worked for Alice anyway.

Eventually I reached a détente with my parents, and we started talking again. As mad as they had been with me, I think they'd actually been angrier at the paper that ran the item. At the Sunday press briefing, the Press Secretary skewered reporters for ignoring the long tradition of the media leaving the private lives of presidential offspring out of the news. He even handed out copies of the Letter to the Editor former First Daughter Margaret Truman Daniel wrote the *New York Times* in 1993, in which she begged reporters to leave Chelsea Clinton alone. I stood in the wings, watching him do his soapbox thing. "I'll read part of the late Mrs. Daniel's letter aloud, for emphasis." The Secretary cleared his throat. "The reporter, quote, 'made a list of all the circumstances that would be embarrassing to a shy, thirteen-year-old girl thrust into the Washington limelight, and used them as his framework. His article bordered on child abuse. My sympathy is with Chelsea, since I too was hauled off to Washington—at the age of eleven, when my father was elected to the Senate, and incarcerated in the White House when he became president.' End quote." The Secretary dropped his sheet of paper on the podium and glared into the corps. "Any further questions?" He was met with silence and swiftly moved on to release news of a shiny new clean-energy initiative. Validated, I happily scooted back to my room.

Before dinner Monday night, my mom showed up at my door. She looked rested and presidential, once again. "Audrey, can we talk for a minute?"

"Sure." I swung the door wide. My mother filed in and took a seat on my desk chair, and I hopped onto my bed, hugging a pillow.

Mom started with a tense smile. "What you did wasn't okay for a bunch of reasons. But I'm sorry for losing my cool on Sunday. It might've been the morning, but it was the end of a long day for me."

"Apology accepted. I *am* sorry for creating problems."

My mom studied my face. "It's not like you to act out. Is everything okay?"

I had so much to say in response that I didn't know where to start. Debra leaving. Fighting with Quint and falling for him too. Being treated like a little kid. Not having any privacy or space. Missing my Minnesota friends and my normal life. Madeline being mean and everyone else at Friends being suck-ups. And lingering hurt feelings from being shipped off to live with Harrison because my parents had better things to do. I had lost almost all the things that made my life mine, and I was clinging to what was left.

I decided to start telling her about all this. "Well...not really. Things haven't been the greatest at Friends." I hugged my pillow a little tighter as I opened up. "There's this girl, Madeline, and—"

"Oh, Madeline. I believe I'm well acquainted with her

grandfather." Mom smiled wryly and sank back into the chair. "I'll bet *she's* been welcoming."

I nodded and rolled my eyes. "Totally." I paused to think of what I wanted to say next, but then Mom's phone started buzzing. She picked it up from her lap and stared at the screen.

"Then my only friend transferred to Hogwarts," I said, testing to see if she was still listening.

My mom actually nodded, her index finger scrolling something on screen. I sighed.

"Sorry," she said, turning off the screen and looking up at me. I was about to start talking again when her phone buzzed again. Her hand reached for it.

"That's it, really," I said, disappointed.

Mom glanced up from the phone to smile at me. "I'm sure she's just jealous, honey. Try to ignore her." *Really helpful, Mom.* "Anything else?"

Might as well throw this in, before the phone interrupts me again. "I am super upset that I can't go on the class trip."

Now she sighed. "Do we really have to get into that again? I just don't think it's a good idea."

I shrugged. "Fine." What was the point of trying to talk to her?

Mom stood up from the desk chair and ruffled my hair. "Well, I'm glad we talked." *Not really—more like you read your emails and selectively listened.* "I think it's time for family dinner. Sound good?" I nodded and followed her downstairs. The olive branch of a family dinner was nice, but part of me was disappointed that she didn't try a little harder to talk to me. Were my feelings really such a pain for her to think about? Maybe on the surface things were back to normal, but underneath I still was simmering with anger and hurt.

⚜

On Tuesday, Madeline started blabbing about another party she was going to have over the weekend. She made a big point of listing who to invite, including Quint but not including me. *Great.* But then Quint randomly showed up during my lunch, turning around my day. "How come you're at early lunch?" I asked as he sat down at my loner, I mean VIP, table.

"My fourth period got turned into a study hall today because Dr. Swanson is out sick. I sneaked out to say hi." That made me blush.

As I took a bite of my sandwich, one of the cafeteria chefs, Estelle, walked past. That reminded me of Alice's friend Thomas transforming into "Estella" for a sneaky visit. From that, the idea randomly popped into my head. *Brilliant.* Once I finished chewing, I asked Quint, "Why didn't you come to the party I had when I first started at Friends?"

"Party?" Quint furrowed his brow. "What part—oh, I remember."

"Yeah, there's only been one *successfully*," I interrupted, rolling my eyes.

"I had to visit my grandfather that weekend. He broke his hip. Why?"

"Well," I said, drawing out my words. "It occurs to me that you've never seen 1600."

"Of course I've seen it." He grinned.

"You know what I mean. Inside."

"Noooo," he asked, raising an eyebrow. "What are you getting at?"

"Maybe it's time you visit." I smiled at him, in what I hoped was a flirty way.

"Are you serious?"

"Totally. I can make it happen." *Maybe I should have him over before he spends the weekend hanging out with Madeline.* "Tomorrow," I added.

"Are you sure that's a good idea? Don't you need to ask your parents?" Quint adjusted his shirt collar.

"Sure, I'll ask tonight," I lied. "They won't care, I promise." *They won't care because they won't know.* I knew it was risky, especially after the fight with my parents last weekend. Technically, I still was grounded—whatever that meant for a person who rarely socialized. But a little voice in my head was telling me to fill what was empty—and I couldn't say no. "So are you game?" I pressed.

"Yeah." He shrugged. "I've always wanted to see the inside."

"Okay, so plan on it tomorrow." Lunch was almost over, so I started packing up my bag. "I'll email you tonight?"

"Sounds good." Quint stepped aside as I walked to the recycling can. I tossed my juice bottle in with a satisfying smash. "See you tomorrow!" I waved brightly at him, and hurried inside.

I sat in the last row of my math class and pulled out my tablet, hiding it on my lap under the desk. I opened email and scrolled through my archives, looking for an updated contact list. People constantly are joining and leaving the White House staff, so contact sheets are updated weekly. I found the list, and jackpot: one of the Visitor's Office names, Melanie Pinter, was highlighted in blue, which signaled a new employee. I clicked on her email hyperlink and composed a message, flagged status urgent:

Hi Melanie,

I am writing because I need to meet with a class-mate after school tomorrow. We have a very important assignment due for our music-history class. I feel it would be easiest for me to do so at the White House. Could you please enter his name in the security system: Quintus Roberts. You should have his info on file from my movie party. Also, my mother approved this message.

Thank you,
Audrey Lee Rhodes

Shortly after I got home from school, I had my reply:

Miss Rhodes,

I have made the necessary arrangements for Quintus Roberts to visit the White House tomorrow. Your security detail will be informed.

Best,
Melanie Pinter

I felt a little bad, taking advantage of the fact that a lower-level person might not know that I couldn't just write "My mom approved this message." The process for me having visitors is a lot more complicated than a simple email. I could've begged my parents for permission to have Quint as a guest, but I didn't want them trying to shut our friendship—or whatever it was—down. Plus, that whole being-grounded thing. Anyway, the plan was turning out to be way easier than I anticipated; probably because it rested on tricking the staff and not sneaking boys in wearing drag, Alice-Roosevelt style. Lucky Alice hadn't had to deal with metal detectors and background checks.

At 1600 that night, I emailed Quint and said to meet me at my locker after last period. Then I made a special trip down to the kitchen. Maurice was cleaning up at one of the sinks. He wiped his hands on his chef's jacket as he walked over to me. "To what do I owe this pleasure?"

"I was wondering if I could stock up on some cookies." On Sunday I'd polished off all the ones in my stash.

"Certainly." Maurice hustled over to the cupboards, returning with a big bag of cookies. "Debra's special recipe. These should hold you over."

"Thanks!" I headed upstairs, stopping to grab a few cans of soda. I was all set to entertain.

Chapter 17

I kept refreshing the screen of my phone during Health and Wellness, urging the numbers to creep up to 3:15 p.m. I was half thrilled about getting alone time with Quint, half worried about getting caught. I bounced my legs nervously, rattling Naveen in front of me, who actually turned around multiple times to give me dirty looks—a first, considering how smarmy he always was to me. I rolled my eyes, even though he couldn't see me.

"Audrey? You're rolling your eyes. Do you disagree about the average length of the menstrual cycle?" Ms. Whidbey, the Health and Wellness teacher, was staring at me. The rest of the class turned around to look at me too. Half the people were smirking.

"Um, no." I blushed. "There was something in my eye."

"All right. Well, cycles do vary anyway, so thank you for providing me with a teachable moment."

When class ended, I shot out of the room and toward

my locker. Once I rounded a corner, I saw Quint standing in front of my locker, drumming away at the adjacent one. He had earbuds in and his eyes were closed as he felt out the rhythm. My heart beat a little faster as I walked up to him and gently pulled one of the buds from his ear. "*Hi*," I whispered.

"Hey!" Quint smiled and dropped his arms to his sides. "Am I dressed okay and everything? For the White... your house?" He was wearing the Friends' boy uniform: pressed khakis, scuffed loafers, and a white polo with the Friends insignia embroidered on the breast pocket. The polo was snug, perhaps a half-size too small, suggesting that either he'd been growing or his housekeeper had shrunk it in the wash.

"You look fine," I assured him. "In case you're wondering, my parents probably won't be around. They're so busy." Quint raised his eyebrows but didn't say anything. I grabbed my jacket and a few books from my locker, then slammed it shut. "Ready?"

Quint nodded and followed me toward the door at which Hendrix was waiting. "Agent Hendrix, you know my friend Quint Roberts. He's coming over to work on a history project."

"I thought it was a music project?" She looked stern.

My face flushed. "Uh, yeah...*music* history."

"Something outstanding from that class you two were in *last term?*" Hendrix pressed.

"Independent study," I hastily replied. *She so knows that something is up.* But Hendrix didn't say anything else. *Thank you, Secret Service circle of trust.*

The drive back to the White House was almost silent. Not what I expected. Quint didn't say a word but compulsively tapped out drumbeats on the armrest. I started to wonder if this was all such a great idea. The possibility of running into one of my parents gnawed at me. *Why hadn't I planned this for a time when they were both out of the country? Or at least the capital?* But I needed to spend time alone with Quint before Madeline's weekend party.

We pulled up to a little gate south of the Eisenhower Executive Office Building because I had a visitor. Hendrix showed Quint's school ID to the guard, and we pulled ahead to a second gate, closer to the White House. Hendrix got out and opened the car door, and Quint and I scrambled out. He showed his ID again and walked through a metal detector. On the other side of it, an aide stood with a badge for Quint. "Here you go," she said cheerily, placing the lanyard around his head like a lei. "Welcome to the White House." Hendrix escorted us up to the Residence—thankfully bypassing the West Wing.

"Where will you be working?" Hendrix asked.

"My room." I quickly added, "Because that's where the computer is. I might show Quint around a bit first?"

Hendrix nodded and listened to her walkie-talkie. "Sure. Your father is at the lab and your mother is in Cabinet meetings."

"Okay, thanks." *Awesome.* Cabinet meetings always take forever. I shifted my bag onto my other shoulder and turned to Quint. "Shall we?"

"Thanks," he said shyly. I led him down the Center Hall. I wanted to get him upstairs as quickly as possible to avoid any run-ins with people who would know that his unchaperoned visit was fishy. "This is the China Room, that's the Diplomatic Reception room, the Map Room is over there, and the kitchen's over that way too. The main kitchen, where the chefs are. There are kitchens upstairs too, for our family. But we don't bother to use them much. This way, upstairs." *Chop chop.* I led Quint to the staircase. He moved slowly, his head whipping around to take in everything on the ground floor before we headed up. "Come on!" I said, hoping I sounded cheery and not like an impatient tour guide. I wanted to get us upstairs before anyone could question his visit. Especially Denise.

"Isn't there a bowling alley?" he asked tentatively.

Going down to the basement would take too long. "Yeah, but it's closed right now," I lied. Quint looked disappointed. I kept moving toward the stairs to the first floor.

Upstairs, we only paused briefly in the Cross Hall. "This is the 'State Floor' because it's where all the receptions are. For diplomats and stuff. The Green Room, Red Room, and Blue Room are all here. And the East Room and the State Dining Room. Plus, the Family Dining Room, where we sometimes eat as a family. But that is *so* rare." I was getting out of breath, racing through my descriptions of all the rooms. *I should give the tour guides more credit. This is hard.* Quint looked longingly toward the closed doors lining the hall. "We can take a quick peek if you want."

"Yeah!" he said, his face brightening. I felt a pang of guilt for not being able to treat him like a *real* visitor. But since he'd never been over before, he wouldn't know better. We dashed from room to room, popping inside so he could look around. Quint was most interested when I showed him the dumbwaiter in the Family Dining Room's pantry. Then we headed up the stairs again to the second floor, stopping again in the landing.

"This is where the private Residence starts. Although the rest of the White House gets thousands of visitors each day, most don't come up here. We live on this floor, and upstairs there's the Solarium and a game room and the greenhouse." Quint nodded. "There are more bedrooms than any family would ever need, except maybe the Roosevelts. The Lincoln

227

Bedroom's over here. Come on." I motioned for him to follow me. "It's the only super-interesting bedroom."

We checked it out and then headed over to my room. "My room's the 'Yellow Bedroom.' A lot of First Daughters lived in it, like Caroline Kennedy, Amy Carter, and Chelsea Clinton." I plopped down on my rug. It felt too weird to sit on the bed with Quint there. "Have a seat!" I said brightly. Quint took off his shoes at the door, then walked over and sat down across from me on the rug, leaning against my bed. He shifted uncomfortably and fiddled with the buttons on his shirt.

"You didn't have to take off your shoes," I said.

"Habit, I guess. My mom doesn't let us wear shoes in the house. Anyway, you have a white rug." He stretched out his long legs in front of himself. "It's so weird, being here. Like, surreal."

"Tell me about it. And I live here."

"What's it really like? I wish we could see the bowling alley. What about the movie-screening room? Someone said there was a flower shop? You must never be bored."

"Kind of the opposite, actually," I said, fiddling with some strands of the rug. "The novelty wore off fast. Those rooms aren't as cool as they sound." I tugged at a loose strand and pulled it free. "Sometimes I want to order a pizza that won't arrive cold from having to go through security, you know?"

Quint laughed. "That's too bad."

"I guess it's fun if you like to bowl alone," I joked.

"I thought you said that was closed?"

Right. I blushed. "Right now. Maintenance."

Quint nodded. "Do you miss Minnesota?" he asked.

"Constantly!" I answered. We fell into an awkward silence, so I saw no reason not to break it by bringing up the awkwardest topic: Madeline. "Um, how's Madeline?"

Quint blinked at me. "I don't know. What do you mean?"

I stared at him. "Aren't you guys a thing now? At least you were at that party?" Quint gave me a blank stare. "After Friends won Science Olympiad?" I added helpfully.

"I have no idea what you're talking about," he said. "Seriously."

I frowned. "So you didn't kiss her."

"No! Why would you think that?" I had turned away from him, so he crawled down the rug to sit directly in front of me. "Did someone tell you I did?"

"I heard Stacia and Claire talking about it in class, to Chris. They had a picture of you guys sitting next to each other…"

"People can share a couch and not make out, you know," Quint said. "And it's not like Stacia and Claire are the most reliable sources."

Oh. *Of course.* Madeline probably ordered them to fake gossip to make Chris jealous. My face flushed. "I'm an idiot, aren't I?" I asked sheepishly. "They were probably trying to tweak Chris."

"Probably." Quint echoed. "Is this why you've been acting so weird around me lately?"

I nodded. "Uh-huh."

He shook his head. "You should've asked me about it. Because I was starting to think that you didn't want to hang out with me." Quint sat back, biting his lip.

"No, that's not how I feel at all. I was upset because—I like you," I said quickly, knowing the many ways *like* could be interpreted.

Quint picked one meaning of *like* and went with it. "You *like* me?"

I blushed and stayed silent, staring at the carpet.

"Because I *like* you," Quint said quietly.

My head snapped up, whipping my ponytail against my cheek. "I guess I *like* you too, then." My heart started doing calisthenics in my chest.

Tentatively, I scooted toward Quint until I was inches away from his face. I looked up into his eyes. Their closeness scared me. *But if Alice could date Edward* and *Arthur while she lived here…* I touched the *WWAD* bracelet on my wrist. Alice would tell me to go for it. I took a deep breath to quell the fluttering in my chest.

"There aren't security cameras in here or anything, right?"

he whispered, leaning toward me. I could feel his words on my lips.

I shook my head slowly. "Nope."

"I can't believe I'm in the White House. With the First Daughter. You," Quint murmured.

"Believe it," I said, then closed my eyes and leaned in to kiss him. Quint reached up and put his hand on my cheek, and then our lips met. *This is totally the best moment of my life*. My fingertips and toes and everything surged with energy as his mouth pressed mine. I'd written off kissing when my mom got elected. Now it wasn't just becoming a possibility again, *but it was happening*. In 1600. *Whoa*.

Finally, I felt like I was eating up the world.

Chapter 18

W e'd been sitting on the floor for an indeterminate amount of time, *kissing*, when someone knocked on my door. I pushed back from Quint immediately, sending him slamming into the side of my bed. We stared at the still-closed door, frozen like statues.

"Audrey?" My mom.

"*Oh no no no,*" I whispered. I clamped my hand over Quint's mouth to stop him from saying anything. "*Under my bed. Quick.*" I helped roll him under. To whoever decided to loft my bed: *Thank you.* I yanked the dust ruffle down around the side. "Coming!" I stood up and checked that no part of Quint stuck out, then walked over and opened the door. I was shaking.

"Hey, Mom. What's up?" I leaned against the door frame, blocking the entrance. I crossed my fingers behind my back, hoping my mom wouldn't notice my smeared lip gloss. Or my mussed hair. I thought of Alice writing about girls with messed-up hair being considered scandalous. *Luckily, bed-head isn't so suspicious now.*

"Just wanted to check in with you. It's going to be a long night for me—they scheduled a Homeland Security briefing at six. I have a little break in my schedule right now." I glanced over at my alarm clock. 5:15 p.m. *Can I really hide a boy under my bed for forty-five minutes, with my eagle-eyed mom in the room?*

"Well, can I come in?" My mom laughed. I realized I was still blocking the doorway.

"Uh, I was kind of in the middle of some homework," I feebly tried.

Mom glanced at my clean desk and my turned-off laptop. "Really? It doesn't look like it."

I figured it would be better to let her in at that point, so I opened the door wide and backed into the room. *Karma really has it in for me.* My mom strode in, walked right past the bed, and plopped down in my desk chair. I shuffled over to the bed and sat down cautiously. *I hope I don't crush Quint.* My heart was beating so hard I was surprised my mother couldn't hear it. She picked up a book from my nightstand. I rubbed my sweating palms on my uniform skirt.

"So you're reading—" Mom was looking straight across the room, at the doorway, when her voice stopped. I followed her gaze to a scuffed-up pair of size-10 men's loafers sitting to the side of the door. *Uh-oh.* "Whose shoes are those?" my mom said slowly, before she jumped off the chair and walked over to the door. She reached down and picked up one shoe, shaking it toward me.

"Um," my mind went blank of any reasonable excuses. *Mine?*

"Is someone else in here?" Mom marched over to the closets, whipping both doors open. Every step she took shook me with dread. Seeing nobody inside, she turned around and walked back to me, now standing directly in front of where Quint was hiding. "These are *boys'* shoes—" Without warning, she squatted down and pulled up the dust ruffle. Quint offered my mother a meek half-wave.

"WHO IS THAT?" she yelled. "Come out! Immediately!" She turned so she could see both the tall teenage boy army-crawling out from under the bed and me hyperventilating on her other side. "You've got a lot of explaining to do, Audrey. Start *now* by telling me *who* this is. Hiding under the bed." She raised her arms up to her head and threw them back down to her sides. "In my daughter's bedroom!"

I wedged myself between Quint and my mom before I tried to spin the situation. "Mom—this is my friend Quint. He came over after school to work on some stuff. I cleared it with the Secret Service and the Visitor's Office and everything, I swear. I just didn't have a chance to tell you."

"Right. And he's hiding under your bed so I wouldn't see him because…?"

"Because I realized that I forgot to tell you! I thought you'd be mad!"

"You're darn-well right I'm mad. You *know* you are not allowed to have boys over unsupervised. Even if you tell us first!" She huffed and stuck her hands on her hips. "I might be busy, Audrey, but I'm not senile. I know sneakiness when I see it. This whole situation reeks of you taking advantage of your father's and my schedules to break the rules. And on top of everything else lately…" She shook her head. "Wait a minute. You're supposed to be grounded too!" *Now she remembers.*

Quint was quivering next to me. "Mrs.—Madam President, can I say how sorry I am?" he piped up. His eyes were bugging out of his head, and a bead of sweat rolled down his temple. "I had no idea you had rules about visitors. I thought you knew I was coming over. I absolutely meant no disrespect."

My mom's voice softened. "Apology accepted. I'm not angry at you, Quint." She only has to hear someone's name once before she starts using it every time possible in conversation—politician's trick. "It's unfortunate to meet under these circumstances. I hope you'll forgive my out-burst, Quint, and not take it personally." She turned back to me and glared. "I'm going to call up the Secret Service now

236

so we can arrange for Quint to get home." She walked over to the house phone and dialed. I took the opportunity to whisper to him.

"I'm so sorry. I had no idea something like this would happen."

"Really? Because it sounds like you knew I wasn't allowed here," he hissed back. "And now the *president* is kicking me out!"

"I didn't think—"

"About anyone but yourself. Thanks." Quint refused to look at me. "I bet the bowling alley isn't even closed." I didn't have to nod for him to know he was right. This visit had been all about me. Superselfish. I felt lower than whale crap at the bottom of the sea.

My mother hung up the phone. "Audrey, stay in this room. Quint, please gather your things and I will escort you downstairs." He nodded, shoved his feet in those tattletale shoes, and grabbed his bag. Neither of them said good-bye to me as they left the room, and the door slammed behind them.

As soon as I heard them walking down the hall, I ran into my bathroom and turned on the shower. I figured the longer I stayed in there with the door locked, the longer I could avoid the inevitable fight with my parents.

When I finally emerged, pink and sweaty from the steam,

they were waiting in my room with somber faces. I walked into the room without saying a word. I fiddled with the drawstring on my sweats while I waited for them to start yelling.

"This pattern of acting-out has got to stop, Audrey," my mom said, stone-faced. "Why are you doing this?"

"If I'm so difficult, why don't you send me away to Harrison's again?"

"That's ridiculous. We're a family," my dad said. *We don't act like it, lately.* I stood silently in front of them, staring at my feet. The worst part was—I didn't want to be sent away. I wanted to help my parents, like Alice sometimes did. But I didn't want to feel trapped anymore. I wanted a life of my own. One with school trips and boyfriends.

My mom sighed. "What you did—sneaking in your friend—was *not* acceptable. We can't have any more mischief, especially not in the press." She paused. "We're taking away your phone and disabling your wireless Internet access, until next Monday. Your right to have visitors is suspended indefinitely—and everyone at the Visitors Office and the Secret Service knows it too. Memos have been sent."

I couldn't believe it. *My phone and First Friend Laptop are all I have.* I shook with anger. "This is cruel and unusual punishment. You already *physically* took me away from everyone I love. Now I can't even email my best friend? Or

Debra? You can't do this!" I pleaded, tears streaming down my face.

My mom clutched her head with her hands, shaking it back and forth. "How else are we supposed to get through to you? Whatever this was a cry for, it wasn't okay. Actions need consequences."

Dad added, "I'm sorry, Audrey, but you've pushed us to the limit."

"This is already a prison. Now it's like solitary confinement," I moaned. "Excuse me for thinking I might be allowed to be normal and have a friend over." But nothing would change their minds.

My parents had a State visit to Mexico scheduled for that Friday. They debated canceling because of me, but ended up asking Harrison to fly out to stay while they were gone. How deliciously ironic is it that during my exile they called in one of my favorite people in the world to monitor me? Nothing can feel like punishment when Harrison's around.

However, he'd barely set down his luggage when he launched into an uncharacteristically parental discussion with me. "Obviously your mom told me why she needed me to come out and stay with you." He held me at arm's length and frowned. "What's going on? This isn't the Audi I know! She wouldn't be driving her parents crazy like you've been."

"I'm not trying to drive them crazy," I insisted. "I'm trying to stop myself from *going* crazy. Let's review: I'm trapped in the White House except for when I'm at Friends. In public I'm expected to be seen and not heard, or I'm getting attention for things I don't *want* to be getting attention for." I paused, biting my lip. "I know I seriously pissed them off, but I didn't mean to. I was trying to fix my life."

"Fix it?" Harrison gave me an *Are-you-serious?* look. "How is wearing a flapper dress to a State Dinner going to fix your problems?"

"Maybe that was flawed logic."

"Or crashing a golf cart?"

"It was an accident."

"*Okaaay*, what about getting caught with cigarettes?"

"I wasn't even going to smoke them!" *Pointing out that I'd been holding on to antique cigarettes to commune with a long-dead First Daughter isn't exactly going to buy me any credibility.*

"Sure, sure. Now explain to me how sneaking a boy into the White House improves your life." Harrison smirked.

"It would've improved it, if I hadn't gotten caught."

Harrison rolled his eyes. "I'm being serious."

I crossed my arms over my chest. "Have you ever done something impulsive, Harrison?"

"Don't try to change the subject, Audi," he chided.

"I'm not changing the subject. Have you ever done something crazy—like, to feel *alive*?" I paused, wrinkling my forehead to think better. "To feel like you were in charge of your own life?"

Harrison's face softened, and he put his hand on my shoulder. "Sweetie, rarely does doing something crazy give you more control in life."

I frowned. "Maybe, but I don't get to decide anything anymore. I was only trying to feel less like that."

"I get that." Harrison nodded sympathetically. "There are things in *my* life that I wish I could control, but I can't." He paused for a few seconds, gazing into space. He cleared his throat and said, "For example, there's nothing I want to do *more* in life than marry Max. But that's not up to me." He shrugged his shoulders, like he was shaking off his emotion.

"But you could in some places—you guys could move to Minnesota, or you could come here! Gay marriage is legal in DC!" I said excitedly, imagining Harrison moving in down the street. Max could come along and be the Cowles to Harrison's Bye. I could escape to their house and hold parties—what was Alice's word, *salons*—for my friends there. *That* would make my life a little better.

Harrison smiled sadly. "We've thought about it. But Max doesn't want to leave his job. And I certainly couldn't replicate mine here." Harrison was the director of the Wisconsin State Historical Society.

"Oh." I frowned. "Yeah, I guess if you want to stay in Madison, you're kind of screwed."

Harrison laughed. "Our life is pretty okay. Do you see what I'm saying, though? Sometimes we have to make the best of our circumstances. Or we have to make sacrifices for the people we love." He hesitated for a minute, before adding, "Look, I know you didn't ask your mother to run for president. It drastically changed your life, not always for the better. I get why you resent the situation at times." He smiled sympathetically at me. "It's healthiest, though, to try to keep things in perspective. Which is asking a lot, and maybe asking you to grow up maybe sooner than you would've had to otherwise. But that's life, kid."

"I guess." I sighed.

He leaned over to give me a hug. "That's my girl. Now we're far from done talking about this or anything else, but do you want to help me drag this stuff up to my *chambers* and then at least find a couple of chairs, preferably not too overstuffed?"

I laughed. "Sure." I grabbed his carry-on bag and led him up the stairs. His flight had been delayed coming in, so it was late by the time I helped him dump his stuff in the Lincoln Bedroom. He always wants to stay in there because of the ghost rumors. I said good night and headed up to my room. No phone, no TV, no Internet—but plenty of books. I picked up one of the new titles some publisher had sent for me earlier in the week, but couldn't focus on the stories. All week, Quint's last words on Tuesday had haunted me: thinking *about anyone but yourself.* Was he right? I understood, now, what a horribly awkward position I'd put him in. I hadn't meant to hurt him or my parents while I tried to help myself. *But I have been a little selfish.* If only they all understood what life was like for me now. Nobody did, except one person. I picked up Alice's diary, and decided it was time to finish it.

November 16, 1902
Diary—

Well, lo and behold: Alice is in big trouble again. Maggie and I, along with some other friends, did head to Benning track last Saturday. After checking for reporters, I proudly stepped up to a bookie and placed several bets. I won plenty, Diary! I shrieked and jumped up and down, clicking my heels, letting out unladylike war whoops. One less dress I have to worry about refashioning for the holiday season.

However, some sneaky camera-fiend at the track

managed to snap pictures of me placing that bet, and now hell hath broken loose. My father's advisers are wringing their hands, crying that this will ruin him politically, because "he has permitted me to become a 'scarlet woman.'" The words of the WCTU biddies, again. Oh, and apparently they have also taken issue with my public gum chewing—the advisers were moaning about that too. Would they rather my breath reeked of tobacco?

Anyway, although the papers reported my bet, they did so as a rumor, and some of my father's friends managed to stop the sale of the photographs and retrieve the images. I asked Edith if I might frame the snapshots and hang them in my bedroom. She frowned and ripped them to shreds. I am a bit disappointed. Betting becomes me.

Also disappointed is my father. After the interest I took in the coal strike and the good work I've done charming Prince Henry, the French delegation, and all those people down in Cuba—he thought I was growing into a real asset for his political career. But now he says he's not so sure if I'm not another publicity fiend taking advantage of his important position. Diary, that stung. His own daughter out to take advantage of him! I profess, some of my greatest memories since

*we became the family in the White House were those
I spent helping my father out. When he said we were
both "Toughs" and could host the French together—
well, moments like that are when I think that maybe I
do belong in this family after all.*

*He remains highly annoyed about the whole bet-
ting debacle and although I've tried to stop by his office
and inquire about politics or philosophy, he's brushed
me off. Have I really crossed the final line? I know I've
said that I want to escape my federal prison, but I wish
to do so on my own terms. Not get sent off in shame
once again. Did I make my fears of another abandonment by my father come true? Please let that not be so.*

*TTOSBT,
Alice*

*December 12, 1902
Diary—*

*What a mess I've made of things lately. I've alienated
my father after working so hard to get into his good
graces; I've let my heart be broken by Arthur Iselin;
and I've even bet a bit too much in poker. The holiday
season should be merry, but I feel bleak. No one has*

been paying much attention to poor me lately at all
of the holiday parties and dinners. I have been bringing Emily Spinach out to play when I can get away
with it, so I don't completely fade into the wallpaper.
I also started eating asparagus with my fingers, while
wearing my elbow-length gloves, until my stepmother
noticed and made a huge fuss. That detail made the
newspaper gossip, which seems stupid. Shouldn't there
be more important things for reporters to write about
than my asparagus-eating habits? The East Coast
isn't freezing this winter thanks to my father's Square
Deal—maybe that's why the press has so much free
time to report on my table manners.

Today I went to Bye's house, my sanctuary, and
visited with her and Cowles until evening. We had a
nice fireside chat, during which she urged me to repair
my relationship with my father. She suggested, in a
gentle way, that it was time for me to find ways to be
rebellious while being a lady. She also said, "Perhaps,
my darling, you need to stop focusing so much on how
you are separate from our clan and more on the ways
in which you can integrate yourself with your family—
even Edith." Loneliness and sadness and self-pity are
like vines, according to Bye, and they have ways of
overtaking whomever they are growing on. One must

cut them off lest they grow unchecked. It reminded me of what the preacher likes to say, "God helps those who help themselves." Maybe they're both right.

To Thine Own Self Be True,
Alice

February 6, 1903
Diary—

Since I last wrote, we celebrated Christmas and I have been to New York and back. Christmas was jolly enough—I slept in until noon and then went shopping on the eve. On Christmas Day, my father gave me a fascinating baby pistol, and I skipped out on church to practice target shooting on the glass garden houses on the South Lawn (they will be removed as part of the renovations, lest you think I was committing a federal offense by riddling them with bullet holes). Like my father, I am quite the shot. I also received an etiquette manual as a gift, which I have grudgingly studied.

I left for New York after the holiday, thinking I needed a change of pace to pick up my spirits. Despite a civil holiday, my parents and I were still at odds. Yet social rounds in New York only made me feel homesick.

In the midst of one dull dinner, I meditated on my last conversation with Bye. Then I had an epiphany—that I must work to find a home within my family. So I sent a telegram to my parents, telling them I would be home to them earlier than expected. I added, "Father: will make self useful as well as ornamental." I hopped the next train to Washington. When I walked in, my family was waiting for me in the reception room. "My darling daughter, my little Tough is home!" my father cried as I entered the room. The little ones ran up to hug me. I said something barbed but witty, to distract everyone from the fact that their welcome brought tears to my eyes.

Later that day, I marched into my father's office. I told him I was ready to be of service to him, to help his political career and stop hindering it. His eyes twinkled in a way that suggested he didn't believe me, but he said, "Go on. Tell me how you'd like to help." Very seriously, I said that I am a real asset when I travel and that I can charm a crowd like few other women can. I wanted him to use "Princess Alice" as an ambassador. As a child, I begged him, "let me loose in your library." Now I begged him to let me loose in the world, and let me spread goodwill for his administration.

And then he gave me permission to go down

to New Orleans for Mardi Gras! I can't imagine anything more enthralling than a real New Orleans Mardi Gras—parties, parades, masquerades, balls, and the like. It will be bully fun. I will be staying in luxury at the McIlhenny home on Avery Island, right where they make the famous Tabasco pepper sauce. I expect I will get to indulge in spicy food again!

The best part is, my father said that this is a test—if I behave myself in the midst of Mardi Gras, he will send me on more trips abroad. Sometime soon, a delegation must go to meet the emperors of China and Japan. If I prove myself reliable and worthy, like I did in Cuba, I will travel to the Orient. I am so happy, Diary—happy that I will be getting a chance to eat up the world, and happy that my father's trust in me is coming back at long last.

To Thine Own Self Be True,
Alice

February 12, 1903
Diary—

I think I may have fallen in love again.

Today was my birthday. The whole clan ate

breakfast together, and I received some presents—a new dress (Alice blue, of course), a new purse (large enough for my four essentials), and some needlepoint materials from Edith. She said she will teach me how to make new pillows for my room. I know what I will embroider on one—"If you can't say something good about someone, sit right here by me."

My father took an hour on my birthday morning to sit in his library and talk with me—talk about great ideas, about great thinkers (whose books he gave me, including more Mark Twain). Someone stopped in while we were speaking, to ask him about some union issue, but Father actually told him he must wait until he was done conversing with me—and that he was busy teaching me to be an ambassador to his presidency. Father said I am the brightest young lady he's ever encountered and how proud of that he is. I had to struggle not to cry (again!), but I succeeded. The sadness I've been carrying around due to all of our scuffles the past few years—it just lifted a little more. He did say that while he knows I will always be high-spirited, if I want to help him I will have to choose wisely how I let my spirits carry me in public. I suppose I can be distinctive without shocking people for the heck of it. Well, most of the time.

I spent the afternoon at Bye's, preparing for a dinner I would hold there for some friends in my social circle. Lila and Maggie attended, and a few Knickerbocker boys. But the most interesting (to my girlish heart) attendee was Nick Longworth. Nick is a Harvard fellow, and like my father, he was a member of the Porcellian Club there. That's why Nick attended my party—my father thought we might enjoy each other's company. I doubt it crossed his mind that I might be less interested in Nick's tales of Harvard life and more in his dashing figure and slick mustache. He's quite a bit older than I am but one of the most eligible bachelors in Washington.

Although I could be a ninny and wax philosophic on Nick's dapper clothing or his sparkling and smart eyes, I won't. Instead, I will tell you that I have met a chap who likes to tell a joke as much as I do, who is known to be an excellent gambler (and he admitted to hearing tales of my impressive winning streaks and begged to see the photographs from the day at Benning), who loves travel and adventure, and who is as passionate about politics as my father. It's not often that I meet someone as tough, smart, brash, and lively as a Roosevelt. Nick is the sort of person who wouldn't be intimidated *from a hunting trip with Father or a night debating politics with Bye.*

And, you know, unlike most people I come across, he never once asked a question about my father. Instead, he wanted to know my opinions, why I loved Twain so, what my tales of Cuba were, and my secrets to gambling success. Me, Diary. He took an interest in me.

I always dream about finding a suitor who has a compatible spirit, someone who likes to be a little conspicuous and a bit renegade. But most of all, someone who will see me outside my father's formidable shadow. Dare I think that I may have found someone like that? I know I have cried "wolf" with matters of the heart before, but I think I might've found a person who can free me from fears of being "poor Alice," who won't help me escape the White House but will escape with me into the greater world, so I can really start living my life. We shall see, Diary.

To Thine Own Self Be True,
Alice

Chapter 19

And like that, the diary was over. I had to set it on my
desk as soon as I turned the last page because I couldn't
stop the tears rolling down my face, and I didn't want to
mess up the ink on any of the pages. *How am I going to sur-
vive without any more of Alice's stories?* I could research her
life, and I definitely would, now that it wouldn't spoil the
diary's secrets. But it wouldn't be the same. It was weird,
but I missed Alice already.

I sat up in bed, sniffling and thinking. The combination
of Alice's diary and my heart-to-heart with Harrison the
night before gave me an amazing idea—how I could use my
situation in the White House for good *and* make myself feel
"useful as well as ornamental," like Alice wrote. Maybe my
actions weren't going to be as free as I'd like while I lived in
1600, but that didn't mean I had to stifle my words. Step
one: get back my Internet access.

"Harrison, I need the Internet to do some homework,"

I whined the next morning over scrambled eggs and bacon in the Solarium.

He peered over his *Washington Post* at me. "I didn't just fall off a turnip truck, Audi." He snapped the paper back open, mumbling from behind it, "I don't want to face your mom's wrath for letting you break the rules."

"You mean breaking *more* rules," I corrected him. "I swear it's for research. I need to write an essay on civil rights. Please let me get a little Wikipedia action in?" I pleaded. "I'll even use your laptop so you can check the history."

Harrison sighed and set the paper down. "Okay, but I will check it—if you stray from homework-y sites, you are in deep crap." I grinned and clapped my hands. "I never thought I'd see a teenage girl clap about getting to do research," Harrison said, shaking his head. "Much less on something history-related. I need to tweet this to my cronies."

I had already jumped up and cleared my dishes to a bussing tray. "I'm gonna go get started if you don't mind."

"Go right ahead. Laptop's logged in and sitting on the desk."

"Thanks!" I took off for the Lincoln Bedroom, taking the stairs two at a time.

The first thing I searched for was "same-sex marriage," which turned up a ton of articles, so I narrowed down what I wanted to focus on: states that allowed it, arguments in support of it, and anything related to human and civil rights. I scribbled useful facts in one of my school journals as I clicked from site to site. The more I read, the more riled up I got. I even downloaded a copy of the Constitution and read it. By the time lunch was ready, I had a bunch of notes in my journal. Enough info for me to write a persuasive essay.

Harrison and I spent the rest of the weekend having a movie marathon in 1600's theater. We couldn't agree on any choices, so we alternated picks—Harrison kept selecting the classics, but it was okay because one was *Roman Holiday*. Not only did it give me some ideas for sneaking off to New York, but Princess Anne reminded me of Alice, and maybe also me. When she talked about her "duty," it gave me the chills. I had responsibilities I didn't ask for, so maybe I had a duty too. I thought more about my essay. Maybe I should revisit the idea of making marriage equality my First Daughter platform.

After we'd already watched four films, Harrison bolted upright in his seat. "My goodness, you're not supposed to be watching *movies*!" He clapped his hand over his mouth in horror. "That was part of the house arrest!"

I laughed hysterically. "I can't believe you let me watch *four* before you remembered!"

"Look at you, taking advantage of me in a senior moment," Harrison tsked.

"Um, you're forty-four. That's too young for that excuse, and you know it," I shot back.

"Please, please, *please* don't tell your mom and dad, though. Seriously." He sighed. "I am the worst prison guard."

"I pinkie swear I won't tell," I said solemnly, holding out my pinkie. Harrison rolled his eyes but presented his, and we linked and shook our hands.

❧

On Monday Harrison flew back to Madison and I went back to Friends. I kept trying to explain myself to Quint—staking out his locker and stalking his class schedule, but he proved strangely adept at making himself unfindable. I sent him long apology emails from the computer lab. I even shoved an apology letter through the vents in his locker, but got no response. It was eating me up inside. I emailed Debra and begged her for advice.

After school, I curled up in bed with my laptop, Internet privileges newly restored. Which was actually a terrible thing, because Facebook was full of pictures of my classmates having fun at Madeline's party—including Quint. He'd even changed his relationship status to "It's Complicated." *As in something complicated with Madeline, maybe?* I guess he'd written me off completely after I got him into trouble last week, and I couldn't really blame him. *I know how Alice felt now when she lost Arthur. And it's horrible. Unbearable.* I collapsed into a wailing heap; this felt as bad as when I had to move away from my crush Paul. Or maybe even worse—I felt like Paul was my Edward, and Quint was my Arthur. I knew which one haunted Alice's broken heart in entry after entry. *Is Quint going to haunt mine now too?*

Eventually, I stopped crying. I washed my face and sat back down to check my email, resolving to stop torturing myself and stay off Facebook indefinitely. A response from Debra was waiting in my inbox. I clicked it open immediately.

To: 'Audrey Rhodes' firstkid@thewhitehouse.gov
From: 'Debra Amesquita' secretagentchef@mail.com
Re: Hello!

Hi Audrey,

I can't tell you how nice it was to get your email. Thanks for your kind words and thoughts about my daughter. We had good news from her doctor this week and are very hopeful! I'll keep you posted.

I'm sorry you're having a tough time with Quint. I know you didn't mean to hurt his feelings. If you've already apologized and told him how you feel, sometimes you simply need to give people space. If I have any advice for when you feel like things are going poorly, Audrey, it's that focusing on helping others almost always makes you feel better about yourself and your problems. It's a good way of taking your mind off things and staying patient. A good book helps too.

Oh, and you *did* inspire my email address. Isn't it great? My grandkids love it. So thank you!

Keep in touch, and take care. I hope I'll be seeing you soon.

Love,
Debra
P.S. I told Maurice that he needs to master my cookie recipes and keep the kitchen stocked with them AT ALL TIMES.

I sat silently at my desk for a few minutes after reading it, absorbing Debra's words. *"Focusing on helping others almost always makes you feel better about yourself and your problems."* It was time for step two of my plan to be a Fido force of good. I pulled out my notes on civil rights and marriage equality, and started to write. When my essay was polished and exactly how I wanted it, I printed out a copy and ran down to the West Wing, to Denise's office. She was bent over her desk, working. I knocked and startled her. She motioned for me to come in.

"Your parents are en route," she said, still glancing down at the papers on her desk. I took a seat in front of her, clutching my essay.

"Actually, I was hoping to talk to you." A framed diploma from Georgetown Law School caught my eye. "You went to Georgetown? Tell me all about it!" It was time to try the elbow-in-the-soup treatment one more time.

Denise looked up, surprised. I noticed at that point that the coffee mug on her desk had a Georgetown seal. *She must adore her alma mater. Jackpot.* Denise actually grinned at me. "I did. I absolutely loved my time there. Undergrad and law school."

"You must've always wanted to be near the capital, I suppose."

Another rare Denise smile. "You got it."

"What was your *favorite* part of being a student there?" I leaned forward, resting my elbow on her desk.

"Hmm. I don't know if I could pick one thing. I had wanted to come to Washington, DC, since I was your age, when I first got interested in politics and government—"

Denise went on to tell me about the Model UN club she founded at her high school and how she was student-council president, and how she started reading the *Washington Post* at age nine. Back then, she drew her own political cartoons as a hobby. I nodded and oohed and ahhed and channeled Alice and her Aunt Corinne as best I could. Denise ate it up.

After fifteen minutes of the treatment, I felt like it was time to make my request. "I'm getting interested in politics too, Denise. The nut doesn't fall too far from the tree!" I grinned. "Do you think I could work on creating a platform?"

"I certainly think so!"

I held out my essay. "I wrote an opinion piece, actually, on civil rights."

Denise glanced at the papers I held out. "Like a school essay?"

"Basically," I said. "But I want other people to read it."

"Let me—" The phone buzzed, interrupting her. I could see her interest in me fading.

"Can I put it online?" I asked quickly.

"For school? I don't see why not." I couldn't believe how cool she was being about it.

"Well, more than school. Do you want to read it first?"

"Mmm-hmm." Denise was typing something into her phone. "Leave a copy, and I'll try to." She motioned to a stack of memos and file folders on her desk. "Sorry, Audrey. Now I need to return that call. Nice chatting."

"Yeah, it was." I meant it too. The elbow-in-the-soup treatment, when it worked, was amazing. I'd never seen Denise act that human before.

I went back upstairs and started figuring out how to get my essay out in the world. I figured after the talking-to from the press secretary, the big papers would never run a letter from me. Better to think of a blog. I knew from hearing all of the staff talk about it that *Squawker* had a huge readership. *Perfect.* It only took a few minutes on their site to find a submissions email address, and shortly after I clicked Send. I smiled and sunk back onto my pillows. *Debra's right. It feels good, trying to help out other people.* Perhaps my parents would see me taking an interest in political causes for once and feel proud of me, like Teddy Roosevelt did of Alice when she talked to him about that miners' strike. Maybe I could be an asset for my mom too.

Chapter 20

When I booted up my laptop the next morning before school, an email was waiting in my inbox from someone with a *Squawker* address:

Hi Audrey,

My name is Tina Pressler, and I'm an editor at Squawker. This is a great essay that you've written, and it's admirable that you want to use your platform to advance this issue. We would love to run it, and since you are reaching out to us, we don't consider this a violation of your privacy. Can you confirm that (1) posting this will not go against your parents' wishes, and (2) you are certain that you would like to publish an opinion piece like this. Once something goes online, there's no going back!

Let me know (in writing) what you decide, and thanks for thinking of us.

Best,

Tina

That was a no-brainer—of course I wanted them to run it. I quickly replied back:

Hi Tina,

Thanks for emailing me. No overnight regrets here—I still want to use my platform or whatever for this issue. Please post it!

Thanks,

Audrey L. Rhodes

I couldn't wait to see it online, and for people—including my mom—to realize that I had something to say.

In the middle of third-period science, Hendrix opened the classroom door and stepped inside. "Excuse the inter-ruption, Dr. Powell, but I need Audrey for a few minutes." Dr. Powell got the same mildly worried look on his face that every teacher got whenever I'm called out of class—like he's wondering, *Is the president okay? Is there a situation? What could it be?* Ironically, it's almost always for something like me needing to be reminded to take antibiotics or an aide dropping off homework I forgot. (Now *that's* a perk.)

I followed Hendrix out the door, slouching in the gaze of the rest of my class. Hendrix's mouth was set in a stern frown, which broke as she asked, "Have you, by chance, contacted any media organizations lately, Audrey?"

That. A nervous chill crept up my back. "I might've," I said tentatively.

Hendrix nodded. "Which?"

"*Squawker,*" I said. "I sent them an essay. A helpful one," I added.

Hendrix exhaled sharply. "I see. I think you might need to head home to explain that to some other people right now. Hang on a minute," she said, and listened to something on her earpiece. "Yes, we're definitely going to take you back for a bit. Do you need to get your bag?"

I nodded, then opened the door and walked back into the room as the whole class turned to stare at me.

"Everything…okay?" Dr. Powell asked.

"Yeah, but I have to go." I left it at that, picked up my bag, and hightailed it out of the classroom.

As soon as we got to 1600, Hendrix ushered me straight to the Oval Office. As we walked down the West Wing hallways, a few staffers glanced up at me from their monitors. A couple shook their heads at me, but one or two others looked…surprised, and maybe a little proud. Hendrix opened the door to the Oval Office and stepped aside for me to walk in. My mom wasn't at her desk, but Denise stood to the side of it, speaking with a few staffers. She pulled her reading glasses down her nose to peer at me as she walked in. "I need a moment alone with Miss Rhodes, please." The staffers nodded and filed out of the room. "Audrey, come over here. I have something I'd like for you to read." Denise spoke very calmly, but that vein was already popping on her forehead. Silently, I walked over to join her next to the desk.

On the computer monitor was *Squawker's* home page, of course. The top story, the one that always got a ridiculously huge red headline, was: TWEEN FIRST DAUGHTER MAKES BOLD POLITICAL STATEMENT. Two thousand comments already. I gulped.

"Let's read this bold political statement, shall we?" Denise's voice carried a sarcastic edge, which freaked me out. She scrolled the mouse down. The article was accompanied with a picture of me on the golf cart, in front of the marriage-equality protestors. *Oh, crap.* It read:

WHY I SUPPORT MARRIAGE EQUALITY AND
YOU SHOULD TOO

Squawker received this exclusive editorial from First Daughter Audrey Lee Rhodes. Formerly most known for Bikinigate and various gossip items about her alleged White House shenanigans, Miss Rhodes here takes a stand on a hot-button political issue: marriage equality. Her essay is reprinted here in its entirety and without editing:

First Daughter Alice Roosevelt carried a copy of the United States Constitution in her purse, and perhaps that's why she described herself as a supporter of freedom. As the current First Daughter, I will keep a copy of the Constitution in my bag too. I recently read it in its entirety, and I think the most important ideas it talks about are equality and freedom. For everyone.

Being in this role has taught me a lot of things, but most of all it's taught me to respect the principles on which this country was founded. The fact that people in America are treated equally and fairly is what makes our country great. But how can we say that we are respecting the Fourteenth Amendment if we don't respect the civil rights of our LGBT citizens? Marriage is a civil right, and right now we're denying it to a lot of U.S. citizens.

I'm addressing this issue for personal reasons—because someone very close to me doesn't have the right to marry his life partner. It's not fair that their commitment can only be recognized informally. I might not have a lot (or any) power as First Daughter, but if I did, I would make sure that all Americans have the right to civil marriage, regardless of sexual orientation.

Even my personal hero, Alice Roosevelt, back when people were not as open-minded about sexuality as we are today, supported the rights of people of all orientations. She knew what I know: that the Constitution means freedom for *all* people, not just some.

"Well," Denise said after a long pause. "This has made quite a day for us. And it's barely noon." She looked up at me, fidgeting to the left of her chair, and sighed. "All of the major news networks are reporting on this. As you can imagine, many groups have already weighed in on your comments. Unfortunately, we were hoping to announce the new climate-change initiative today, but that has to wait. All thanks to you." Denise narrowed her eyes. "You've single-handedly shifted the focus of the entire media to two topics: same-sex marriage, and *you*."

"You told me I could put my essay online! I even gave you a copy beforehand!" I pointed at the stack of pages on her desk. It was much taller than last night, with my essay probably buried somewhere in the middle.

"What?" She shook her head. Her voice rose as she

continued, "You said it was for school. Anyway, right now I need to work with the press staff to figure out how to spin this PR kerfuffle, courtesy of one very irresponsible First Daughter." She waved me toward the door, her manicured nails making angry swipes through the air. "Go up to your room and wait for your parents. And, for the love of God, stay off your email, and the phone, and passenger pigeons or smoke signals or whatever else you'd use to hijack the conversation. How your mother puts up with you, I don't know."

Tears welled up in my eyes. *I asked for permission for this. It was supposed to make my mom respect me. Not make her life harder.* But I knew it wasn't the right time to say that—and I didn't want to spend another minute around Denise, who clearly hated me again. I ran out of the room before anyone could see me break down and cry.

Chapter 21

I hid out in my room for hours, curled up on my bed and clutching Alice's diary. *My mom will probably read my essay and be disappointed in me like Denise was.* I only wanted my parents to give me independence the same way Teddy Roosevelt did for Alice—a little freedom to live my life and speak my mind. I wanted them to see me as a person and not their problem. I slammed the diary shut and buried my head under the pillows.

I still was hiding from the world like that when someone knocked. "Yeah," I called, the pillows muffling my voice. "Come in." I didn't budge.

"Audrey?" It was my mom; I could hear her shoes clicking toward the bed. "Are you okay?"

I sat up, red-faced and static-haired. "Sure," I said unconvincingly.

"I think we need to talk," my mom said, sitting down next to me. She left a shopping bag leaning against the bed, then kicked off her low heels and tucked her feet underneath herself, leaning back into my pillows.

"You mean fight?" I snorted.

"No, I mean *talk*, actually." I sat up as my mom cleared her throat. "I owe you an apology. For *a lot*."

My head tilted in line with my surprise. "You owe *me* an apology? For what?"

"First of all, Denise shouldn't have confronted you about your essay. I've already spoken to her about that. She needs to focus on my office and not my family, even when they overlap." My mother smiled and brushed a strand of hair off my cheek. "I think she misinterpreted your intent. I know you gave her a copy beforehand." So Denise wasn't totally evil—she'd told my mom the truth about that. Mom continued, "I read and reread your essay a few times this afternoon. I was surprised by how smart it was. I *shouldn't* be surprised because I know my daughter is a bright girl." To that, I smiled. "Why don't you tell me why you wrote it, honey?"

"This is not a trick question? Like, *explain yourself*?" I leaned away suspiciously.

"I promise not. I'm ready to listen to you." She pressed the button on her phone to power it down. "No interruptions."

"Okay." I took a deep breath. "When Harrison visited, we talked about a lot of stuff, including marriage equality.

It seems so unfair that he and Max can't get married. I don't think it should be that way in our country. Then I realized I have the ability to say that to people because I'm your kid. Or maybe I have a duty to speak out." My mom was nodding like she got what I was saying so far. "I'd been trying to figure out how to make the best of this crappy situation—I mean, make being in the White House worthwhile. Debra once told me that helping other people is a good way to make yourself feel better." I paused. "I wanted to help people by writing that. People like Harrison and Max."

"That's admirable. But why *has* it been so hard for you here? I know you've been hurting lately, and I'm sorry I haven't done enough to figure out why."

The words tumbled out. "I don't get a lot of privacy or freedom at 1600. People don't seem to want me to grow up. I don't have many friends at school because it's hard to be seen as *me* and not the First Kid. I can't go on the class trip to New York or anything. You and Dad are so busy. I had Debra, but she had to go away. I'm lonely here, even when I'm surrounded by people. Nice people, like Hendrix and Simpkins." I paused to catch my breath. "No one under-stands me, except—" I reached over to grab the diary. It was time to show it to her. "Except Alice." I handed the journal to my mother, who carefully flipped it open.

"I can't read this—who does this say it belonged to? Is that *Alice Roosevelt*?" She gasped.

"Yeah. It was her journal." I scooted closer to point out the inscription. "I found it in a closet, along with those old cigarettes and a few pictures of her. By the way, that's why I had cigarettes on the roof. I found them with the diary. They were Alice's."

"All the more reason you shouldn't touch them, if they are over a hundred years old," my mother said, but she was chuckling.

"I know—I kept them safe, for the Smithsonian." I waited while she paged through the journal. "I read the whole thing. And for the first time since we moved into 1600, I felt like someone understood how it feels to be here. To live in a house that's not your home. When there's so much attention on you but none of it is *for* you. Someone totally got me without me needing to say a word. It's not like I've been talking to an inanimate journal." My mother nodded, so I continued. "Alice was crazy. She danced on roofs and raced cars and sneaked in boys and scared visitors with her pet snake. She still fell in love and lived her life even if the fishbowl made it hard. She actually liked the attention. So I decided to try to do the same for myself. Alice was my guide."

"So that's why you wore the dress, drove the cart, took

cigarettes up to the Promenade, sneaked in your friend...," my mom said slowly, adding up the misdeeds on her fingers.

I blushed. "Yeah. Original, huh?"

My mother smiled. "You were, actually." She pulled out the picture of Alice and ran her fingers over it. "Both of you. I wish I'd listened to you sooner." She put the picture back and picked up the journal again. "I'm impressed and a little touched. It makes me happy that you care about people like Alice. I read a lot about Eleanor Roosevelt when I was your age."

"She wrote about Eleanor in there a few times. You should read it!" I reached over and tried to find a page that mentioned Eleanor. "Alice was awesome. Not only because she did all kinds of wild stuff, but because she cared about people and freedom and fairness and her family."

"This all makes so much more sense, Audrey." My mom smiled sadly. "But you know, Alice was living in a very different time."

"I guess," I said.

"The press then wasn't like it is now. There was no media cycle. There was privacy for the First Family in a way that no longer exists. The First Daughter making a political statement was received a lot differently then, and less widely. Alice had the benefit of being a First Daughter in the days before celebrity."

"She *was* the first big celebrity," I added. "Which is cool."

"Very cool." My mom pursed her lips, figuring out what she'd speechify next. "You have the power of being in the public eye now, Audrey. And with power comes responsibility, whether you asked for it or not. Now you have a great responsibility to use your visibility wisely and respectfully."

"Mom," I interrupted. "You just plagiarized *Spider-Man*. 'With great power comes great responsibility' is a line from the movie."

"Not the *p*-word!" my mom exclaimed, laughing. "Please don't tell on me. Well, I guess you know that lesson already. My bad. That's what you say, right?"

I suppressed the urge to groan. "Um, yeah. Do not use that in public."

She smiled. "I'm sorry my career has made this responsibility necessary for you at such a young age. I hope you'll forgive me for the burdens I know I've placed on our family. If I didn't truly believe that I have a chance to do a whole lot of good in the world as president, I never would have put you in this situation."

My throat felt tight, so I swallowed hard over the lump and nodded.

"I think we need to have better communication with each other. Let's start with you telling me how you feel and what help you need from me. I'll do the same. Dad and I will work on making things easier for you. We can try to give you more access to a 'normal' life. But while I want you to let your voice be heard, can we agree that we'll at least talk about how you'll use it, first? I promise I'll give you that freedom, but I need to know beforehand what you'll be saying."

"That sounds good," I said. "I'm sorry if my essay screwed anything up for you."

"Nothing that can't be fixed. This will blow over when the next story breaks, and you drew attention to an issue that I care about too. I always wanted to address it during my administration, and now you've brought it to the forefront."

"Did Harrison say anything?"

"He told me I needed to listen to those within the White House a little more closely on that topic. One person in particular. I think he was very touched." I smiled.

"One more thing," she said, untucking her feet and reaching to lift the shopping bag. "It's crazy how this is working out, what with you having Alice Roosevelt's diary. Serendipity at work." She pulled an old throw pillow out of the bag, holding it close to her chest. "I noticed in your essay how you mentioned Alice a few times. So as a little peace offering, and to show you that I'm listening now, I asked the museum if we could take something of hers back to the White House while we're in residence." She turned around the pillow and held it out to me. Embroidered across the front was: IF YOU CAN'T SAY SOMETHING GOOD ABOUT SOMEONE, SIT RIGHT HERE BY ME. "Alice Roosevelt made this and had it on display in the White House."

"I know!" I grabbed the pillow and ran my fingertips over the embroidery. "I read about when she decided to make it!" I looked up at my mom, who was grinning. "This is awesome, Mom. Really awesome."

"I'm glad. Take care of it—it's a national treasure."

"Oh, I will." I gave her a huge hug.

"I'm going to go finish up some work, but you can come and get me whenever you want to eat dinner. Your dad's on his way home too. We'll be eating together tonight."

"Sounds great." After she left the room, I put the pillow on display in the armchair by my window. I couldn't stop smiling whenever I looked at it.

Chapter 22

I walked into first-period history the next morning to a standing ovation from my classmates, and it wasn't sarcastic. "Way to go, Audrey," Mei said. "That essay was pretty cool." Our teacher, Ms. Branch, had written across the whiteboard "CIVIL RIGHTS" and "THE 14th AMENDMENT." The desks were all arranged in a circle, which meant that it was going to be a discussion day.

"Audrey, you've given me a great introduction to talking about the Constitution and civil rights. I wasn't going to start teaching it until the spring, but I want to keep the dialogue you started going. Would you mind sharing a little with the class about why you wrote that piece?"

I blushed, but I wasn't embarrassed. I didn't mind having so much attention on me when it was for something I had done. "Sure, I don't mind." I put down my bag and started talking.

At lunch, I was about to sit down at my loner/VIP table

like usual, but then I saw Stacia looking up at me. She was actually smiling, so I took a deep breath and walked over to her.

"Can I sit here?"

"Sure!" she said. The kids she was sitting with scooted over to make room. As I set down my tray, she said, "I wanted to say thanks. Your essay made my sister so happy. Like, knowing that someone in the White House cared about her rights like that. It was pretty cool you wrote it."

I grinned. "I'm really happy to hear that." I liked this—getting attention for being me, not my mom's daughter.

As I bit into my sandwich, Quint walked into the lunchroom. He scanned the room and his eyes locked on me. I set down my PB and fancy J and turned to Stacia.

"I'll be right back." I got up and walked over to Quint. "Hi," I said. I wanted to tell him that whatever "It's Complicated" meant, it was cool with me. It would suck if he was complicated with Madeline, but I'd rather be his friend than his nothing.

"Hi," Quint said. He looked embarrassed. "I need to apologize for something."

"Good—so do I." I smiled. "Let's head outside for a minute." We stepped out into the empty, freezing courtyard. Thankfully, Hendrix and Simpkins stayed within the double doors. "Me first?" I asked.

"Sure," he replied.

"I'm sorry I put you in a bad situation by sneaking you into 1600—my house. It wasn't fair to you. It was selfish of me. I'm sure it sucked to have to meet the president under those circumstances. Even if the president is just my mom."

"No kidding." Quint laughed. "But thanks for apologizing."

"I would've apologized sooner if you hadn't been avoiding me," I teased. *It feels like we're going to be friends again, at least.*

"Yeah, that's what I was going to say I'm sorry for. It was lame to ignore you like that."

"Thanks." I took a deep breath and balled my fists. "Also, um, whatever 'It's Complicated' means, I'm totally fine with it. You're my friend, and I want you to be happy. I won't be weird about it or anything. I promise."

Quint raised an eyebrow. "Wait, what?"

"I saw that your status is 'It's Complicated.' I figured you went to Madeline's party and—"

"No, it's not like that at all!" Quint laughed. "Madeline is my *friend*. I've known her since pre-K. We were talking at her party—about you, actually. Even if she's still bitter about the election and your mom, she gives me good advice."

"Are you serious?"

"Yup. You've gotta give up your paranoia about me

liking Madeline! By the way, you guys should try to put politics aside and be friends. I'm working on her about that."

"Well." I paused. Having friends at Friends would be nice—even Madeline. "I'd like that." *Maybe the next time I see Madeline, I'll try the elbow-in-the-soup treatment on her. It's worth a shot.*

"The president doesn't actually hate me, right? Because I want your mom, no matter who she is, to like me. Your dad too." My pulse quickened. *It feels like we're going to be* more *than friends, again. Dare I hope so?*

"Seriously?" I couldn't hide a smile. "So even though I'm kind of a screwup, you still like me?"

"You're not a screwup. Especially with that op-ed you wrote. That was supercool."

"Supercool," I said slowly, grinning.

"I like girls who write supercool stuff," Quint said, leaning in toward me.

"Lucky me," I said. I stood on my tiptoes to reach him for a kiss. It was equally awesome as the one we shared in the White House. *Hendrix and Simpkins are just going to have to get used to a little PDA on their watch.*

When I got home from school, an envelope was sitting on top of my laptop. "Audrey" was written on it in my dad's handwriting. I ripped it open and pulled out a folded letter. A few postcards tumbled out from the paper—one of Times Square, one of the fountain at Lincoln Center, and one of the Statue of Liberty. I squealed even before I read it:

Dear Audrey—

We know this year has had its ups and downs. We're both very proud of the young woman you're becoming, though, and we appreciate the sacrifices you've made so we can follow our dreams. We want to do the same for you. To start, we're going to make all the necessary arrangements so you can go on your class trip to New York. Get excited!

Love,
Dad and Mom

P.S. We're also working on getting easier security clearance for some of your school friends to visit, starting with Quint. The open-door rule will still apply!

I couldn't believe it. I wasn't sad at all to abandon my half-baked plans to sneak away to NYC. So long as I got a little freedom and the occasional taste of a normal life, I was okay with playing by the rules. I pirouetted around and around my happy Yellow Bedroom, stopping to grab Alice's diary from my nightstand. More than anything, I wished I could tell Alice what had happened. *I am eating up the world!* That was when I got my next great idea and pulled out one of the blank journals I'd never bothered to start keeping.

Epilogue

Hi Fido,

First, don't get upset that I called you that. I was a Fido too—still am, as I'm writing this. (In case you don't know what I'm talking about—Fido is the acronymish nickname kids at my DC school gave me. FIrst DAUghter—FI DAU—Fido, like the dog name?) Anyway, if you're reading this, you've moved into 1600 too, and you are indeed a Fido. (Or a Fiso, I guess. But the Yellow Bedroom's seen more girls than boys in the past couple of centuries.) Congratulations to your mother or father on his/her victory!

Living at 1600 can be awesome—I don't need to sell you on the swimming pool, the bowling alley, the movie theater, or the chocolate shop. Oh, the chocolate shop. Get those keys to the cookie tray ASAP. (Have you fully explored the basement yet?) However, 1600

...an also be totally lonely. I had a hard time with the loneliness the first year I lived here. Maybe you have some siblings to keep you company, or maybe you're an only child like me. Either way, it can get rough. I didn't always deal with my feelings so well. (Ask the archivist for some of the tabloids from during my mom's administration.)

I had nobody to commiserate with until I met Alice Roosevelt. She was a First Daughter too—back at the turn of the twentieth century when Teddy Roosevelt was president. I didn't actually meet her, of course—she'd been dead for decades by the time I moved in—and I don't mean that she was haunting the place either, although I've heard rumors about ghosts in the Lincoln Bedroom. I met Alice when I found her journal hidden in the dining room closet. The Smithsonian has the original, of course, but they printed and bound a "facsimile" copy for me. I put that back in the diary's hiding spot, in case you're interested in reading it (and you should be, because Alice was awesomesauce). Look for a funky floorboard and the words, "Eat Up the World." You'll figure out what that means.

Even though Alice and I lived in the house a hundred-plus years apart, we shared similar experiences.

Meeting Alice was the best thing that could've happened to me, and it helped make my life at 1600 livable. She helped me find freedom. Don't worry. I'll explain the whole story behind that in here.

Because Alice's diary helped me so much, I'm keeping this journal for you. Paying it forward. Maybe someday you'll read this and my words will help you sort through the confusion of life as a First Kid. I hope so. And if I'm still around, feel free to contact me. We Fidos need to stick together.

Best of Luck!
Audrey Lee Rhodes

Author's Note

Alice Lee Roosevelt Longworth was a real person—a fascinating and funny one. She was born on February 12, 1884, the only child of Theodore Roosevelt and his first wife, Alice Hathaway Lee. Sadly, Alice's mother passed away two days after giving birth. Alice spent her early years living with her Aunt Bamie, whom the family called "Bye." After her father remarried to Edith Carow, Alice returned to live with her father, stepmother, and five half siblings—  plus lots of pets (including a monkey and a badger named Josiah). Theodore Roosevelt became president in 1901, and once in the White House, Alice became both a First Daughter and the nation's first celebrity. She traveled the world to help her father's administration, enchanting the press and occasionally shocking them too—like when she jumped into a swimming pool fully clothed. Alice's wedding to Nicholas Longworth (that's right—she really did marry Nick!) brought thousands of guests to the White House to watch her, wearing an Alice-blue dress, chop into her wedding cake with a sword. Alice and Nick had one child, a daughter named Paulina. Alice acted as an adviser to her father throughout his political career, and she continued to be a strong presence in Washington's political and social circles after his death; she was well known for her outrageous behavior and her legendarily sharp wit. It's not for nothing that her nickname became "The Other Washington Monument." Alice died on February 20, 1980, at age ninety-six.

Rightfully, Alice is the subject of many great nonfiction books. This is not one of them, because the Alice you found in these pages is a fictional creation. I tried to capture the real Alice's vivacious spirit, deep curiosity, lively wit, and fierce intelligence in my character Alice. I also described things Alice really did (like practicing yoga and smoking on the White House roof) and incorporated things she actually said (like telling an interviewer that she supported the rights of gay people). Although I tried to stay faithful to what happened in real life, when it came down to good fiction versus factual accuracy, fiction won. Therefore, please treat my Alice, as well as her friends and family, as characters.

Books and online resources, a few helpful DC friends, and a tour of the White House grounds helped me imagine Audrey's world. I aimed to make that setting as realistic as possible, but occasionally I stretched the truth or invented details of contemporary White House life for storytelling purposes. I like to say that the White House in *When Audrey Met Alice* is 100 percent accurate to Audrey's experience of being a First Daughter—and is plausible in terms of the real-life White House.

I hope you enjoy this work of fiction and that it inspires you to learn more about the White House and the real Alice Roosevelt. I've created a guide, *Alice, For Real*, which explains more clearly what's true and what's made-up in *my* Alice's diary. It also gives credit to the nonfiction sources that provided me with fascinating and juicy details about the real Alice's life. In particular, the works listed in the bibliography by Stacy Cordery, Michael Teague, and Barbara Kerley were invaluable resources, and I cannot recommend their books enough to anyone who wants to know more about Alice. You can find *Alice, For Real* at books.sourcebooks.com/when-audrey-met-alice.

Works Cited

Works cited directly in Alice's story:

Cordery, Stacy. *Alice: Alice Roosevelt Longworth, from White House Princess to Washington Power Broker.* New York: Penguin Viking, 2007.

Kerley, Barbara. *What To Do About Alice?* New York: Scholastic Press, 2008. [for young readers]

Teague, Michael. *Mrs. L: Conversations with Alice Roosevelt Longworth.* Garden City, New York: Doubleday & Company, Inc., 1981.

Other excellent books, articles, and online resources about Alice, her friends, and the Roosevelt family:

"Countess Cassini, Former Washington Belle, Now a Refugee and Dressmaker in Italy" *The New York Times* 29 October 1922.

Donn, Linda. *The Roosevelt Cousins: Growing Up Together, 1882–1924.* New York: Knopf, 2001.

Felsenthal, Carol. *Princess Alice: The Life and Times of Alice Roosevelt Longworth.* New York: St. Martin's Press, 2003.

Kimmelman, Leslie. *Mind Your Manners, Alice Roosevelt!* Atlanta: Peachtree, 2009. [for young readers]

Sagamore Hill National Historic Site http://www.nps.gov /sahi/index.htm

Books and websites about the White House:

Edwards, Susan. *White House Kids.* New York: Harper Perennial, 2000. [for young readers]

The White House's official website www.whitehouse.gov

The White House Historical Association website http://www .whitehousehistory.org/

The White House Museum website www.thewhitehouse museum.gov [an unofficial virtual reference]

White House Historical Association. *The White House: An Historic Guide.* Washington, DC, 1962.

White House Historical Association. *White House Words: A Style Guide for Writers and Editors.* Washington, DC: The White House Historical Association, 2011.

More links and resources are available at the author's website, www.rebeccabehrens.com

Acknowledgments

Thanks first to my wonderful agent, Suzie Townsend. Without her insight, support, and skill this book would not be in your hands. Thanks also to the entire team at New Leaf Literary. The agency doesn't just represent writers, but truly nurtures them. In short, they're the best.

Thanks to Aubrey Poole, my fantastic editor, whose vision and enthusiasm has turned this story into a real book. I am so grateful for the care she has shown Audrey and Alice—and me. Thanks also to everyone at Sourcebooks for copyediting, designing, marketing, publicizing, and selling my book so expertly. I am very fortunate to be a part of the Sourcebooks publishing family.

I'm lucky to have some of the most generous, intelligent, and well-read friends, and I sure took advantage of their help (and at least one couch) to write this book. Many thanks to the following for their opinions, expertise, and occasional moral support: Heather Alexander, Megan Drechsel Tomson,

Ellen Tarlow, Kiki Aranita, Annabel Oakes, Kim Paymaster, David Wade, Emily Radford Ryan, Shane Ryan, Ruth White, and Jessica Stewart.

I wouldn't be the writer—or the reader—I am today without the influence of many excellent teachers, librarians, and booksellers. Thank you for letting me loose in your libraries, as Alice would say.

Thanks to my parents for their encouragement and unwavering belief in me, and to my sister, Beth, for always being a boon companion. And most of all, thanks to Blake for encouraging me to create and dream. I wouldn't have done it without you.

About the Author

Rebecca Behrens grew up in Wisconsin, studied in Chicago, and now lives with her husband in New York City, where she works as a production editor for children's books. She loves writing and reading about girls full of moxie and places full of history. *When Audrey Met Alice* is her first book. Visit her online at www.rebeccabehrens.com.

What *Would* Alice Do?

To find out more about Alice Roosevelt and the real life events the inspired the journal entries in *When Audrey Met Alice* visit the Educators page at Sourcebooks.com.

Available for download:

Alice, For Real
A behind-the-scenes look at writing Alice's diary. What's true and what's invented? This annotated edition of the journal entries from *When Audrey Met Alice* provides readers with an inside look at the sources, quotes and historical events that shaped Alice's fictional diary.

When Audrey Met Alice Educators Guide
A Common Core Curriculum aligned educator's guide for Grades 5 and 6 as well as tips for struggling readers and enrichment for advanced readers. Includes: (1) pre-reading question, (2) comprehension questions, (3) classroom activities, (4) a bibliography for further research, and (5) a list of standards.

Women's History Month Lesson Plan

Alice Lee Roosevelt Longworth was a fascinating and funny woman. It's not for nothing that her nickname became "The Other Washington Monument." Rebecca Behrens captures Alice's vivacious spirit, deep curiosity, lively wit, and fierce intelligence in the pages of *When Audrey Met Alice*. Alice's mottos were To Thine Own Self Be True and Eat Up The World. When presented with all the challenges of adolescence, today's young reader could do a lot worse than asking herself: What Would Alice Do?